Tales of Tie-Ins

Emily Martha Sorensen

Tales of Tie-Ins
Copyright © 2019 by Emily Martha Sorensen
Cover and internal art by Emily Martha Sorensen

All rights reserved. Printed in the United States of America.

ISBN: 978-1-949607-58-1

http://www.emilymarthasorensen.com

Also by Emily Martha Sorensen

Wicked Witches of Restva:
Black Magic Academy

Fairy Senses:
Fairy Eyeglasses
Fairy Compass
Fairy Earmuffs
Fairy Barometer
Fairy Pox
Fairy Slippers
Fairy Lunchbox
Fairy Icepack
Fairy Stopwatch
Fairy Toothbrush
Fairy Perfume
Fairy Crown

Dragon Eggs:
Dragon's Egg
Dragon's Hope
Dragon's First Christmas
Dragon's Fire
Dragon's Song
Dragon's First Valentine

Comics:
A Magical Roommate
To Prevent World Peace

Picture Books:
Tabby, Tabby, Burning Bright

The End in the Beginning:
The Keeper and the Rulership
The Fires of the Rulership
The Magic or the Rulership

Trilogy of a Teenage Werevulture:
Trials of a Teenage Werevulture
Trifles of a Teenage Werevulture
Weredodo Sleuth

The Numbers Just Keep Getting Bigger:
Twenty-Four Potential Children of Prophecy

Not Quite a Harem:
Not Quite a Curse

Magical Mayhem:
To Prevent World Peace
To Prevent Chic Costumes
To Prevent Clear Paths
To Prevent Smart Choices
To Prevent Warm Welcomes
To Prevent Cute Mascots
To Prevent First Place (prologue)
To Prevent Fresh Starts

Short Story Collections:
Worlds of Wonder
Magic and Mischief

To Candice,
who is a very fun person
to hang out with.

Thank you!

Table of Contents

Ogre in Boots 2
An Alternate Solution to the Sleeping Curse 8
Puss in Oops 9
Entrance Interview 10
The Weeds within the Rulership 12
The Secrets from the Rulership 16
The Numbers across the Rulership 23
The Novice at the Rulership 33
The Painting like the Rulership 34
Fairy Feet 36
Fairy Fingers 39
Fairy Stink 40
Dragon's Dawn 42
Dragon's Yowl 46
Trials of a Teenage Shapeshifter 48
Triumph of a Teenage Werevulture 49
Trials of a Teenage Zombie 58
One Silly Chatterbox That Won't Stop Talking 60
Three Little Stones That Said the Wrong Thing ... 64
Four Hardened Criminals on a Dangerous Street ... 72
Six Shiny Silver Coins and the Ridiculous Ruckus
They Caused 76
Seven Shameless Scamps Looking Pitiful 85
Thirteen Years After a Sister's Wedding 86
Fifteen Problems in One Hundred Words 87

Author's Notes 88

Tie-ins for the

Wicked Witches of Restva

series

Ogre in Boots

Horinwa was just sitting down to his usual breakfast of snake egg omelets and hemlock syrup when he heard a loud, insistent whamming on the front door. Annoyed, he got up to go see who it was.

On the way, he cheerfully entertained the notion that it might be a Normal stupid enough to believe that pestering a wicked witch was a good way to get a curse put on somebody they didn't like for free. He had gotten a few visitors like that over the years. He always found them to be amusing test subjects.

On the other hand, it might be someone else after his daughter.

If I have to put down another assassin from those sore losers who pass for teachers at Black Magic Academy, he thought darkly, *I'm going to lodge an official complaint.*

So his daughter had been the pride of the school. So she'd managed to keep a horrifying secret hidden from them for well over a year. So she'd outwitted them all and escaped. They really had to learn to have a sense of humor about such things.

He fingered a charm in his pocket, one he kept ready all the time just in case, and flung open the door, ready to face whatever was waiting for him.

There was no one.

"Ahem!" a voice called from below.

He looked down. A tom cat with long, thick whiskers stood on his front porch, lashing his tail. Oddly, the tom cat was standing on his hind legs. Even more oddly, the cat was standing awkwardly inside a pair of oversized boots.

"My name," the cat said grandly, "is Puss."

Ogre in Boots

"No, it's not," Horinwa said.

The cat looked nonplussed. "Excuse me?"

"That's a name used for female cats. You're clearly male."

"W-well, take that up with the human family who adopted me!" the cat sputtered.

"Mm-hmm," Horinwa murmured. He was already bored with this conversation. "I don't lift curses on enchanted princes. If you keep on pestering me, I'll cast a new curse on you, though." He turned to shut the door.

"I'm not a prince!" the cat yelled.

"A helpless bystander, then." Horinwa kept on shutting the door.

"I'm an ogre!"

Horinwa paused. He glanced idly down at the cat through the sliver of openness that remained between them. "Oh?"

The cat stood tall and preened his whiskers proudly. "A human, indeed! I'm a magnificent ogre. Greater and mightier than any such puny beings!"

"Uh huh. You realize you're a cat now, which means you're smaller than me."

The cat's whiskers wilted. "Well . . . yes, but that's temporary."

"Is it, now?"

"It is. Because you're going to break the curse on me."

Horinwa laughed out loud and shut the door.

He headed back to the kitchen to finish his omelet. He would have to heat it up again now, and Rulisa wasn't home to make it simple, more's the pity. He missed having a fire witch around the house.

It wasn't that Horinwa didn't know how to perform temperature magic. Of course he did. As a former teacher of Kraken Institute, it would have been ridiculous for him to not know the basics of any field. But that branch of magic tended to come easier to fire witches than any other element, and Horinwa was a water witch.

Of course, the fire witch he missed the most of all wasn't his daughter. It was his deceased wife, Welsa. Horinwa sighed moodily, sitting back at the table and poking at his cold omelet.

An irritating caterwaul howled from outside.

Horinwa plugged his ears and muttered a soundproofing spell, but it only muffled the noise a little. Wind witches were better at spells than water witches, just as water witches were better at brews.

If he had a torrent of water, he could soundproof the cat . . .

He got up from the table and fetched a bucket of dirty dishwater from the kitchen that he hadn't yet bothered to dump outside. Then he headed for the front door.

The tom stopped mid-cauterwaul. "Now, as I was saying —"

Horinwa dumped the contents of the bucket over the cat. The sodden feline shrieked in horror. With a smile, Horinwa snapped his fingers and sent the cat reeling backwards across the fields at a rapid pace. Back, back, back, back . . .

He chuckled and slammed the door. The booted tom cat would be miles away by the time he stopped. No doubt he would take the hint and go off to pester some other witch who was both closer and a little more amiable.

But the tom cat was back in the morning.

"Now, as I was saying —" the irritating feline began as Horinwa stepped outside his back door to fetch a bucketful of water from the well.

He ignored the chatter, plunged his bucket into the well, and marched back to dump the water onto the cat. When he did, it showered around the tom, leaving a bubble of dryness around him.

Horinwa paused. "You've seen another witch."

"I have, yes."

"From the looks of things, a wind witch."

"Indeed."

"Then *why*," Horinwa asked with exasperation, "didn't you just ask *that* witch to help you?"

The cat preened his whiskers, looking aloof. "I have my reasons. Now, I want you to turn me back into an ogre now."

"I can't imagine why you think your desires will affect me."

"I have mounds of treasure back home," the cat said. "I could pay you."

Horinwa paused. As a member of witch aristocracy, he had no particular need for money. Village witches used it, but when a member of witch aristocracy wanted something from a Normal, they tended to simply take it. Still, he couldn't deny that coins tended to smooth over negotiations with particularly well-armed Normals who didn't take kindly to their natural place in the pecking order.

"All right," he said cautiously. "But why would you want *me*, in particular?"

Ogre in Boots

"I have my reasons," the cat said mysteriously.

"So explain them."

"I'm willing to negotiate the payment, but the reasons are my own. And I have an additional condition: you must come to my home to change me back."

Horinwa paused. That sounded obviously suspicious, and he wasn't fond of walking into traps. On the other hand, he'd always survived before, and some of his best brew materials had come from innocently wandering into a trap that he pretended he couldn't see and harvesting rare materials he couldn't have accessed otherwise while there.

Welsa had once yelled at him for walking into an obvious trap by her death-enemy just because it had allowed him to amble through the gardens of her family's manor for several minutes unmolested before the trap sprang.

Oh, true, he still had the scar on his leg from where the cerberus had bitten him. On the other hand, he'd also gotten some clippings from the enhanced poison ivy that grew along the walls, and those had enabled him to invent a superior itching brew.

Horinwa sighed. He missed his wife a great deal, and his teenage daughter, who spoke to everyone with condescension, was little comfort. Rulisa's haughty scorn simply wasn't as fun to provoke as his wife's rage.

He weighed the risks of following the cat. The chances of finding interesting brew materials in an ogre's home weren't terribly high. On top of that, his wife wasn't here to shout at him for his incaution, which stripped most of the entertainment from the prospect.

Still, the house was awfully quiet with his daughter away at school. He was bored.

"All right," Horinwa said affably. "Let's negotiate on the price."

They negotiated for a long time, arguing until both sides were satisfied that they had successfully cheated the other.

"About food," the cat went on, "I intend to forage for myself. If you want to have a food allowance for the days spent traveling —"

"Days?" Horinwa asked, puzzled. "Why would I spend days? I'm going to fly."

The cat looked alarmed. Its eyes grew large, and it stumbled back and nearly toppled out of its too-large boots. "Fly?"

Horinwa laughed out loud. "Yes, fly, you silly tom named Puss. Don't tell me you've never flown before?"

"I'm an *ogre!*" the cat hissed.

"No excuse," Horinwa said blithely. "There's nothing to it. Just try not to fall, because then you'd turn into a dead little splat."

"We're going to walk!" the cat screamed in panic.

Horinwa laughed. "No, no, we're taking the broom."

The cat seemed deeply unhappy when they departed about an hour later, Horinwa's pockets full of empty vials for new samples and full ones of useful brews.

Horinwa could, perhaps, have been more wary, but he was having too much fun to waste energy on worrying. And thus it was that the trap he had halfway expected managed to catch him completely off guard anyway.

As they arrived at the ogre's hut, Horinwa's feet touched the ground, the broomstick clattering beside him.

A hand made of earth exploded up beside him and clenched him tight in its fist.

Horinwa gasped for breath, finding it difficult to inflate his lungs. This artificial hand-shaped rock was much more powerful than he would have expected. *Blast it. He's hired an earth witch to create protective wards against me.*

"Like it?" the cat taunted, leaping from the bag that was still attached to the end of Horinwa's broomstick. The broomstick that was now, unfortunately, several feet out of reach. "I hired a witch to trap you. Your daughter's the one who cursed me into this form, and I owe her payback! She's too far away for me to get revenge on her now, but you're conveniently nearby. And I'm sure killing you will distress her terribly!"

Horinwa struggled against the earth-hand's tightening grip, his blood boiling. A brigand seeking his money or life was an enterprising businessman who he could respect. A fellow witch wanting to make a name for herself by killing someone as powerful as Horinwa was being perfectly rational. An angry customer trying to repay him for tricking them into buying useless garbage was just part of the game.

But going after his daughter? That was beyond the pale.

Nobody went after his daughter and lived.

A gush of water exploded upwards, shooting torrential arcs in every direction. The arcs danced in dazzling jets and plunged down into the earth again, a constant loop of water rushing from the underground river beneath him.

Ogre in Boots

The hand of earth attempting to squeeze Horinwa to death struggled desperately to keep its shape, but it melted into a soggy mass in no time. In seconds, Horinwa was merely covered with mud and sore and bruised.

He lashed his hand out and a hiss of water responded, twisting and twirling around his arm, undulating like a deadly viper as it flew through the air around him.

"P-please," the cat stammered, taking several steps backwards. He stumbled out of his boots, leaving them soddenly strewn in the mud. "I made a mistake. I-it wasn't Rulisa I wanted to hurt. It was somebody else. It was her death-enemy! Yes! It was her death-enemy I was after! That's right, I remember now, ha ha ha ha!"

"Don't worry, I don't believe in revenge," Horinwa told the cat comfortingly.

The cat-turned-ogre began to relax.

He shot the water-viper at the cat and sliced off its head.

"But I *do* believe in killing threats to my daughter," Horinwa added amiably, ambling over to inspect the corpse for potentially useful brew ingredients.

It was a shame about there being no payment. There was a con he wanted to try with jeweled eggs that would hatch into frogs and snakes, and paying an earth witch to turn dirt into gemstones could be expensive. He would rather pay with much-less-valuable coins than from his personal stash of rare brew ingredients.

Still, he'd protected his daughter from an enemy. That was always worth doing. It was a shame she had so many of them. In witch society, the more enemies you had, the more respected you were, so he ought to be proud, but she never seemed to kill any of them herself, so he kept having to do it for her.

Horinwa picked up his broomstick and sprayed the mud off of it. *Well, a good day's work for a wicked witch. If only my wife were here to laugh over it with me!*

An Alternate Solution to the Sleeping Curse

Mildred watched her friend, the kleptomaniac princess, exit the tower. Worryingly, she was whistling with impish glee. "You woke up that girl under the curse? How?"

Topaz shrugged. She pulled out a vial and shook it. "Same thing that worked on my great-grandmother. Revoltingly strong perfume."

"But I thought it took a kiss to break a spell like that," Mildred protested.

The princess chortled. "That was my great-grandfather trying to spread rumors about what a great kisser he was. Now some people think that same curse will get them dates."

From far above, they heard a wail. "Where's my prince?"

Puss in Oops

"I'm the greatest magician in the world!" the ogre bragged.

"Oh, yeah?" Puss challenged. "I bet you don't even know how to change your shape."

"Of course I do!" the ogre cried. "Just watch!"

He turned into a roaring lion, then a marauding elephant. Puss barely escaped trampling.

"Ah," the cat said quickly, "but small is harder. I bet you couldn't be a mouse, say."

"Of course I can!" the ogre roared, and shrank.

The cat waited, salivating.

Then a skunk sprayed him straight in the face.

"Ha!" the ogre howled, doubling over. "Did you think I was stupid or something?"

Entrance Interview

"So, why do you want to attend the Sukanil School of Magical Studies?" High Witch Dal asked, smiling.

"I don't," Rulisa said flatly.

"You don't?"

"No, but it's not like I have much choice. I got expelled from my first school, and I broke the second one I wanted to apply to."

"You broke . . . the school?"

"Yes, but don't worry, it was on purpose. I'm not incompetent enough to do it by accident."

"And . . . what happened at the first school?"

"I guess you could say I broke that, too."

There was a long, long pause.

"We'll get back to you."

Tie-ins for The End in the Beginning series

The Weeds within the Rulership

"Your parents said you were sick," Jontan said to me, holding out a shabby bouquet through the doorway. His fingers clutched around the stems so tightly that they were bending. "I brought you some flowers."

I stared at him dispiritedly from my bed. I had been hiding in my room for two weeks, not staying here because I was still sick, although that was what I had told everybody. I'd had a fever for three weeks, so that had been a convenient excuse. But no. I didn't want to see people because I was terrified they'd notice that I'd started growing magic.

"Thanks, Jontan," I said, trying to sound glad to see him. He was a friend, after all. "You can leave them on my dresser."

He tiptoed into my room, laid the wilting flowers across the top of the piece of furniture, and then leapt back to the doorway as if burned.

I barely kept from rolling my eyes. "You've been in here before," I told him.

"It's not proper without a chaperone now," he insisted.

Honestly. Jontan took the rules of propriety seriously, it seemed. We were both twelve years old, we'd just *barely* taken the oath of childhood, and it wasn't even like he was courting me. If he started acting all formal now, it was going to drive me crazy.

"Are you going to look at the flowers?" he asked anxiously.

With a sigh of annoyance, because after all I was supposed to be sick, I angled myself out of bed and shuffled over to the dresser. The row of wilted flowers stared up at me.

There were filias in it. Yech. They were such an ugly color, all purple-blue, and they meant "loyalty to the Rulership," so using them was like showing off. Jontan loved the flowers, though, so he had probably included them just because he thought they were pretty. The rest were inna blossoms, which I'd forgotten the meaning of, and torron stalks, which meant "get well soon."

Jontan hovered in the doorway, as if waiting for me to say something.

"Uh, thanks," I said. "I hope I get well soon, too."

He kept on hovering.

Oh no! What if he'd noticed some magic I'd used accidentally? Jontan was a stickler for the rules, and landowner use of magic was more than just a rule: it was a law. If I got caught, I could be killed.

"Ohhh, I have a headache," I moaned, saying the first thing that came to mind. "I have to be alone now. Can you leave me?"

"Oh! Oh, sorry!" Jontan jumped back. "Can I . . . can I come back later?"

"Sure," I said. Of course he could come back later. Why was he even asking? His family's land was right next to ours. We saw each other all the time.

Jontan looked a mixture of scared and relieved, and hurriedly waved goodbye and scuttled down the hallway. I heard his feet pound on the way down the stairs.

I shuffled back to bed and put the sheet over my head. I didn't want to get out of bed. I didn't want to see anyone else today. A spark of magic lurched out of my elbow and made the pillow underneath my head more thin and lumpy.

Argh! I spun around to try to get comfortable again. Horrible magic! It was ruining everything!

The slight scent of innas, torron stalks, and filias drifted through the air. Something tingled in my nose, and I sneezed.

Suddenly the odor was overpowering. The fresh smell of the torron stalks was like a whole field during harvest, the perfume of the filias dug underneath it with pugnacious grandeur, and the inna scent was now so spicy that it made my eyes burn. There was something else as well, something like ash or burning . . .

I gasped and flung the blanket off my head. I hadn't set something on fire, had I?!

No. My bedroom looked the same as it ever had. But the bouquet now had a flower I hadn't noticed before. Something grey, and blobby.

Oh, gross, I thought with disgust. *A groverweed. Jontan didn't watch what he was picking, and picked a groverweed.*

I got up out of bed and picked up the whole bouquet to throw it out the window. Maybe the wind could carry the appallingly strong odor away. As soon as my fingers touched the stalks, the flowers shrank.

Argh! I screamed silently.

Wait . . . why were the other flowers smaller, but the groverweed bigger?

I stared at the bouquet for a moment, confused. As my thoughts raced, magic surged from my hand again, and the odor of the other flowers shrank to nothing. The blobby grey flower's persistent ash scent remained the same.

Slowly, I separated the one ugly grey flower from the rest. Had it grown because I'd accidentally used magic on it? Did groverweed grow whenever you threw magic at it?

Nervously, because I'd never tried using magic on purpose before, I tried pushing magic into the groverweed. It unfurled a leaf, and then put forth a petal. The tingling in my arms ceased.

I concentrated harder, and shoved even more into it. Within just a few minutes, the stalk held a long, straggly clump of roots, black petals ringing a head of seeds, and two more buds growing. For the first time in weeks, I felt satisfyingly hollow and empty.

I drew a breath in wonder. All these weeks of misery, all this time of feeling sick, and all I'd needed to do was . . . that?

I spun around and thumped my hand into my pillow. I tried to make it soft and fluffy, and nothing happened. Not even the wrong thing. It just lay there inertly.

I danced around the room in excitement. I was free! I was free!

My bedroom door opened, and Mother came in.

"Did you accept Jontan's invitation?" she asked.

I froze from dancing around the room, and quickly spun the bouquet around to cover the groverweed.

"Wh-what invitation?" I stammered, nervous that she had seen it.

"The inna," Mother said. "That means he likes you. He said he was going to ask you to the social event that's happening at the Brushflower land next week. Did he?"

I froze. I stared down at the bouquet. I knew I was old enough to be courted now, but . . .

This was an invitation?

"I . . . I . . . I'm feeling much better now," I stumbled. "Excuse me!"

I shoved on my shoes, raced out of the room, and pounded down the stairs, carrying the flowers tightly in my hand.

"Raneh!" Mother shouted behind me. "You're twelve years old! You have to wear your hair up in public!"

I paid her no heed. I flung open the front door and thundered down the dirt road that connected our families' lands.

"Jontan!" I shouted. "Jontan, wait!"

He paused, and I caught up to him.

"I didn't realize what you were asking me," I said, panting. "Yes! Yes, I'll go with you!"

Jontan's eyes widened. "Really?"

"Yeah! Yeah, of course I will!"

We stood there, beaming at each other, both of us embarrassed.

"Thanks for the flowers," I added awkwardly. "They were really great."

He ducked his head, and I felt a surge of giddiness. I was going to go to my first social event with a suitor! And I didn't have to worry about magic! And I was safe!

As soon as I got back home, I was going to plant some groverweed in my garden. It was now my favorite flower in the whole Rulership.

The Secrets from the Rulership

A cry went up across Central.

"The Ruler is dead!"

"The Ruler is dead!"

"The Ruler is dead!"

I stared out the window and breathed a long sigh of relief. *Thank goodness. The Ruler is dead.*

It wasn't that I hadn't liked the old man. Quite the contrary; he'd been my mentor for twenty years. If I hadn't liked the man tolerably well, the shrewd old Ruler would have been a fool to make me his first heir. But even he must have been aware that I'd been getting very impatient for his death.

I was forty-three. I wanted to have children at some point. And Lancen and I could not legally get married until after the old Ruler died and I became Ruler in his place.

Well, to be strictly accurate, we could have gotten married at any point — but only if I had been willing to give up my place as a Ruler's heir. And given that I had wanted to be the next Ruler since I was sixteen years old, and Lancen had wanted to be the Ruler's husband and run Central for even longer than that, giving up out of impatience had never been an option we'd considered.

With the Ruler dead, at last I would be able to take the Oath of Rulership, and I would be legally required to marry right away.

No more frantically wondering how much longer I'd be fertile.

No more worrying that some other heir would beat me to the top and become Ruler instead of me.

No more endless chaperones whenever we were together to make sure Lancen and I behaved.

I stared out the window, feeling the breeze on my cheeks, and let loose a loud laugh and beaming smile. Then I composed myself, because of course it would not do to seem glad for my mentor's death, and turned from the window to walk out of the unlocked door of this room that had been my home for twenty-eight years.

I walked up to the top level of the Heart of the Rulership, where most of the Ruler's mathematicians had gathered beside the wall of history. It was part of the Ruler's private quarters, and I had been shown the place several times, but I had never before been here without my mentor present.

Now it, and the rest of the Heart, belonged to me.

Off to the side of the fresco that displayed the Rulership's history were several lines of words: the oath of Rulership.

It was a short oath that nevertheless held serious importance to the world. It would not work for anyone who tried to take it who was not the current Keeper; it was for that reason that I could not have become the Ruler without my predecessor dying.

I drew in my breath and spoke.

"I, Anced, of the Filias family, do hereby swear to be bound to the Rulership. I swear to put the law above my own preferences, and the Rulership above my own life. Should I suffer senility or madness for any period longer than one month, I give my consent to be executed so that another may rise in my place. I swear this as the Keeper of all status."

My status rose around me, almost seeming to dance within me. Joy bubbled up from within my chest. It was finished, then. It was completed. I was the Ruler, at last.

One of the mathematicians opened his mouth to speak, but then Lancen stepped forward.

"It is necessity, of course, that we be married right away," he said gravely, taking my hands. "For we cannot adopt the previous Ruler's heirs until we do."

I nearly laughed at how solemn he sounded. To one who did not know him well, it might have seemed that he did not care at all, but I knew better than anybody that when he was at his most polite and least emotive, he felt a depth of passion far greater than those who did not show restraint.

"We shall be married before the day is done," I promised him, squeezing my fingers around his.

Such speed was not a necessity. I was only required to marry within three months of taking the oath of Rulership. But that was time I neither wanted nor needed, and I was certain that Lancen felt the same.

"As you say, Ruler," he said solemnly, touching the hair piled up on my head with the briefest brush of a finger.

"As I say," I said, smiling.

A Ruler's wedding was, of course, cause for great celebration, and it was held in the largest building in Central, displacing the citizen family who had reserved it months in advance for an oath ceremony. I had spoken to the family personally and watched for signs of defiance, but they had shown no animosity, merely excitement at being given first-row seating at such an important occasion in compensation for their event's postponement.

I paid little attention to the ceremony, lavish and well-planned as it was. I had cared a great deal about the trappings of marriage as a child, but now that I had waited so long, only my husband-to-be held meaning.

Once the ceremony was over, we retired to our chambers at the top of the Heart of Central, finally to be alone together without chaperones for the first time since we had met.

I felt as though my life, which had been pending for decades, was finally beginning.

Many months later, I returned to the wall of history, a place I had not bothered to return to since my oath, since I'd felt that it had served its purpose. I had noticed an odd reference to it in one of my predecessor's notes to me, however, and I had been meaning to see what he had meant by that note ever since then.

On the far right side of the fresco, the beginning, there were images of many strange and wonderful things. There was sunlight being drawn down to run machines. There was liquid being controlled by gesturing figures. There were animals much larger than the tame ones still kept in the rimlands. There were criss-crossing lines that clearly symbolized an unknown something, buildings being lifted into the air by some mysterious means, and many other strange and mystifying things.

All of these images converged to become the next part of the fresco, which showed the start of the Rulership. The world had once been shaped differently, with many bodies of land, but they had all been drawn together by a force called geo. I knew little about it; only that it had once existed, and it did no longer. But I also knew that it had created the Rulership, the land upon which all people now lived.

So the second image showed messy, divergent continents being brought together to form the smooth, beautiful circle of land that spread across our spherical world and now held all people and land animals on it.

The third image showed the founding of Central, the creation of the Ruler's Roads, the growth of the Heart itself out of the ground.

The fourth image was puzzling; it showed many plants growing, including an ancient flower I knew had been called grower's glory, as well as a long-extinct species called rockflowers. I had seen references to both in archaic books, and both had apparently once been plentiful. I had no idea why they had gone extinct long ago.

The final image before the words of the oath, which were carved at the far left, was of seven different men and women taking the oath of Rulership. Their faces were specific and detailed, and I suspected that these had been the first seven Rulers of the Rulership. I didn't know why their faces were on this wall, when none of the Rulers since had been added; I had once asked, and been told that it was impossible to chisel into the stone.

I touched the faces of one of the ancient, original Rulers, tracing his features under my fingertips. *What means did they use to create this fresco, if it cannot be chiseled or shaped now in any known way? Was it geo, the same force that was used to form the Rulership at the beginning?*

But the pictures carved into the wall were not the reason why I was here. I walked to the oath of Rulership itself, ran my fingers down its chiseled-in letters, and reached a small indentation below it, where my predecessor's note had said it would be.

My finger pricked, and I jerked backwards, staring at the blood welling up. There had been nothing to prick it on. How had that happened?

But now the wall was moving. It slid backwards, and then drew down into the floor. I watched with astonishment as an entirely different wall with new words written on it appeared before my eyes. It had been behind this wall of history all along.

If you are seeing this, it means you are the Keeper. Your blood was recognized by the wall. I write this knowing that the blood system is still extant, but it will soon be gone from the world. I am the last Keeper of geo, and it is important that my successors continue to know what I know.

I drew forward, fascinated. So this had been written by one of the previous Rulers — perhaps the last of those whose face was on that fresco. But what did that mean, "the last Keeper"? Every Ruler was the Keeper. That was how it had always been. It seemed strange that he was calling himself a Keeper of geo, too, as "the Keeper of all status" was the Ruler's full official title. Where did geo, that lost force, come into anything?

I read on, hoping for the answers to those puzzling questions.

The first Ruler declared that all knowledge of the systems cycle should be banned from common knowledge. Books about it were burned, and scholars were put to death. In this way, he hoped to prevent the inevitable. But he could not. Lacel is living proof of that.

Hair stood up on my arms. Lacel was the name of one of the ancient Rulers. As far as I knew, she had only managed to be Ruler for a few years before she had died of extreme old age. What had she done that was so important that she would be mentioned by name?

Lacel is a rising Keeper, the text on the wall said. *Removing knowledge of the systems cycle did not prevent it from continuing. She will become an original Keeper, the kind the rest of us are merely echoes of.*

The danger of a rising Keeper is twofold. First: as long as one lives, they will absorb the weaker system until all of it is consumed. Second: once this is completed, they will use that power to create a brand new system.

Because Lacel is rising, I know that the blood system will soon be gone. This means that geo, one day, will also be consumed. I know not what will replace them, but I know that at some point, something will.

The only way to keep a remnant of a dead system is to tie it to the Keepers or the systems cycle itself. So I make this record using the two systems I know, making it so that it only can be accessed by a Keeper, because that is the only way in which it will be possible to access it at all. I make this using blood and geo, and perhaps you who are now the Ruler know two other systems entirely.

The Secrets from the Rulership

Once I am finished with this record, I will send Lacel to the Pillar of the Heart, the remnant of sunstream that will allow her to complete her task and begin the new system.

Whether you wish to keep this secret, or whether you wish to restore this knowledge to all, is your decision. As the current Keeper of the Rulership, you have all power.

It was signed at the bottom with the name of the seventh Ruler.

My mouth felt dry. I could scarcely breathe. What was this? How was I to understand what he meant?

And then I saw, in a hollow near the floor beside the wall I had uncovered, a collection of old, yellowed papers. I walked forward and picked them up gingerly, seeing that they were signed by the name of the Ruler before my predecessor.

These are the names of the systems, as far as I can reconstruct them, it said, and there followed a long list. At the very bottom were the very few that I recognized: *sunstream, blood, geo, agri, enhancement,* and *status.*

My head reeled. Then that meant status was a system? Status, the very foundation of our society, our very currency, would be extinguished someday?

That could not be. It must not be.

I looked up at the wall, and read the whole thing all over again.

One phrase stood out to me: "as long as one lives."

I looked back at the pages, and I saw my predecessor had come to the same conclusion. He had written his thoughts on the back of the last few pages.

If you ever meet a rising Keeper, then they must be executed for the good of the Rulership. Enhancement is the next system that will die, and we cannot survive without it. As it is growing very weak, I think that it might very well come within your lifetime, Anced. Be ready.

I swallowed. I felt sick to my stomach. The necessity of passing death sentences on those who deserved it was my least favorite part of my duties as Ruler. Every week, I dreaded walking to the prison to pass final judgment on those my heirs had found and deemed probably guilty of the very worst crimes.

But I had sworn to uphold the law above my own preferences. I had sworn to uphold the good of the Rulership above my own life. I had agreed to be executed if the Rulership needed it. I could not stay my hand if the same sacrifice was required of another.

I am the Ruler, I thought. *It is my role to facilitate justice, not to question it.*

Slowly, I set the papers back into their place and stepped back from the wall. As soon as I had reached the doorway, the original fresco slid up from the floor and covered it.

I knew I would return. I knew I would be back to study those hidden words many times. I knew that I would share these secrets with Lancen and otherwise kept them hidden, as concealment from the rest of the Rulership seemed the wisest course to prevent panic and instability. I knew that I was in a state of shock, and that it would take me days to process this.

Still, my mind was already made up about what had to be done.

For the good of the Rulership, if a rising Keeper threatens us all, they must be killed.

I was the Ruler. I was predominant. I was justice.

I would do my duty.

The Numbers across the Rulership

"You know, boy," Grandmother said with her hands on her hips, "you wouldn't be quite so irritating if you would take your duties more seriously."

I wasn't sure whether she was talking about my position as a landowner heir or just the theoretical chores in the kitchen that I always avoided, but since I didn't want to talk about either, I simply piled my plate with pastries and gave her a blithe smile. "You make the best pastries in the world, Grandmother!"

"Oh, off with you," she said scowling, but I saw a fond smile cross her face involuntarily as I turned away.

I grinned as I bit into the first of her pastries. Grandmother was always complaining that the harvest had been terrible and there wasn't enough to go around, but she still couldn't find the heart to refuse me when I came begging for kitchen treats. She made them to sell, and they were an important source of income for our family, yet I could always sneak a few out and get nothing more than a mild scolding.

Somehow, she could always find a way to make delicious treats even when there were far fewer ingredients than usual to work with. She was amazing.

This one, for instance, was drizzled with warm caramel and just a hint of flaming hot haj clove jelly for seasoning. Because she had used only a tiny sprinkling, the effect was spicy, yet not overbearing, and so sweet that it made my teeth ache.

Yeah, even in the middle of a food shortage because of magic disappearing, Grandmother could do anything. Surely even the Ruler didn't have food this good.

Thoughts of the Ruler made the smile drop from my face. She had absconded with both of my sisters a year ago, and I was still furious about it. Not so much about Yaika, whose absence made me feel like "Good riddance," but Raneh's absence was intolerable.

Not just because I missed my older sister, either. I *did* miss her, and I wanted her back, and it was hideous that magic had disappeared while she was gone, so there was now no way back from Central.

But it was worse than just that. With both my sisters missing, I was now my parents' only heir. Which meant the burden of going to social events was now falling on me. Not only that, my parents kept talking about me inheriting the land someday!

I did *not* want to think about my parents dying, thanks very much. And who wanted to be a landowner, anyway?

I chomped into the second pastry I had filched from the kitchen and hummed with delight. It tasted like she'd used powdered spikenuts in place of the usual lef flour, and that shouldn't have worked, but it was perfect. Who cared about a food shortage when Grandmother was around? She could do anything.

I didn't want to be a landowner. That was obvious. Landowners had way too many responsibilities. They were supposed to maintain all the buildings on their land, protect their vassals from crimes or inclement weather, assign the best choices of families to tend particular crops or strips of land, and make sure nobody went cold or hungry. And if a landowner failed in any of those duties, they could be charged with the serious crime of neglect and have everything stripped away!

I didn't want to be responsible for the lives of other people. I didn't want that kind of pressure. I didn't even want to bother to *talk* to people, most of the time.

Unfortunately, I didn't really want to be a vassal, either. Vassals had to work hard in the fields, which sounded mind-numbingly boring to me. Besides, they usually had less status to spend than landowners, which meant they couldn't buy as many pastries. And as for books . . . well, vassals were generally more concerned with practical matters of survival than academic or cerebral pursuits.

Grandmother's delicate techniques of pastry-making wouldn't be possible if she had a strip of land she was responsible to tend. Grandfather's esoteric mathematical research wouldn't be possible, either. Father's expertise in house repairs wouldn't matter at all if he was supposed to grow his own food instead.

Even Mother's highly exotic ornamental flowers and herbs wouldn't be practical to grow in a vassal garden . . . no, actually, she would probably still be growing those even if she were a vassal. Gardening was her favorite activity. I couldn't understand why. It was gross and muddy.

The only things I enjoyed were reading books and eating pastries. Which meant I was rather fat, not that I cared. But the older I got, the less everyone around me seemed to think it was acceptable for me to continue living this way.

My parents tolerated my antisocial habits mainly because I was a useful source of information. Anytime a member of my family wanted to know some detail they couldn't quite remember, they'd go to me.

"Hurik, what color of dye do nectarvines make?"

"Hurik, which is the plant that repels wispyflies?"

"Hurik, are the haj cloves at the peak of their flavor before or after the blooms turn brown?"

"Hurik, does squishwood rot when submerged in water for a long time?"

"Hurik, what do chikweeds mean in a bouquet, again?"

I never had enough of my own books to read, so I was always borrowing everybody else's. That meant I usually knew as many of the theoretical details about their own activities as they did, and sometimes more. Of course, try to make me do anything with those pieces of trivia other than share them around, and I'd go hide in my room. I wanted to learn; I didn't want to *do* things.

There was one set of books I never got to borrow, though, and those drove me crazy. Those were the books Grandfather kept in his room. He was a mathematician, and only those who had sworn the oath of mathematics and permanently renounced status could have access to them.

I wanted to know what he knew *so badly!* But of course I didn't want to be a mathematician. That would require *doing* things. So I was permanently locked away from all the fascinating secrets he knew and wouldn't share with me.

Everything had been fine a year ago. But then my sisters had left with the Ruler, both the perfect and dutiful Raneh and the flashy and popular Yaika, which meant all the pressure from my parents was now on me. Worse, magic had died shortly afterwards, which meant there was no way for them to come back.

So now my parents were constantly nagging me to take the oath of status, which most people did on their twelfth birthday.

"Hurik! If you'd just take the oath already, I could send you to the market to do the shopping!"

"Hurik! Everyone else your age is able to hold currency! You realize you're three years late?!"

"Hurik! Would you stop being lazy and contribute to the family?"

You'd think they would be grateful to me for not taking the oath and thus costing us status whenever people disapproved of me for being rude to those I didn't like in public, but noooooooo.

It was hard to say why I didn't want to take the oath of status. Part of it was that I didn't like the idea that people could judge me and take away some of our family's ability to buy things. Part of it was that I didn't want to be sent outside more often.

I bit into a third pastry from my plate as I reached the top of the stairs. Mmmmm! A frizzle pastry! I loved the way those crackled under my teeth.

Mother was waiting for me in my bedroom as I opened the door. Her hands were on her hips.

"Hurik!" she said. "Did you wash any of your laundry?"

"Umm..." I said, trying to delay.

"That was a rhetorical question," she informed me. "I can see that everything you own is still soiled."

"Oh, what a shame," I said, trying to sound convincing. "I guess I won't be able to go to the social event tonight."

"Oh, you *will*," Mother informed me.

I accidentally-on-purpose let a blob of purple haj clove jelly drip onto my shirt and grinned smugly. "Okay. I'll wear this."

Mother did not seem amused. "You're not going to go in soiled clothing."

"Who's going to wash it?" I asked innocently.

"You are."

"Really?" I smirked.

"Yes, really. Because if you don't, I will personally see to it that you leave this house wearing something from Yaika's closet. I believe she has a lilac bodice painted with adlies and a pale blue outer skirt embroidered with lacewings that would fit you nicely."

I stared at her in horror. "You wouldn't!"

"Watch me."

"But everyone would judge the family!" I exclaimed. "It would reflect on you and Father! People would ding your status at the next social event you went to!"

"No, I rather think we'd both go up in all the other parents' estimations," Mother said with a gleam in her eye.

I panicked. That gleam meant she was serious.

The promise of humiliation was enough to get me moving. I hurriedly shoved the plate of pastries onto my bed and scooped up an armload of clothes off the floor. Then I ran for the stairs.

"Those are all shirts!" Mother called. "You'll want to include something to cover your lower half! Unless, of course, you *do* want to wear one of Yaika's outer skirts —"

I bolted back and gathered up another pile of clothing. Mother didn't fight fair!

The social event was every bit as miserable as I'd expected.

As usual, I sat sulking in a corner, wishing I was at home and resenting that Mother and Father never let me bring a book to one of these things. The fact that no one could magically enlarge rooms anymore meant that these parties were even more unbearable than before, because there was nowhere to sit without people crowded in around me.

A girl whirled across the floor, having finished a dance, and sat down breathlessly next to me.

"Hello," she said, smiling at me.

I gave her a doleful glower.

"Is it because of Jontan?" she asked.

"Huh?" I asked, mystified. "Is what because of Jontan?"

"He danced six dances with Suellen," she said. "That means they're engaged. I heard he used to be courting your sister. I'm sorry."

I really couldn't possibly care less about my older sister's suitors, or lack thereof. I couldn't imagine why she thought him getting engaged to somebody else would bother me.

I shrugged.

"I know," she said in a mournful voice, patting my hand. "He was like a brother to you, and now he'll never be your brother for real."

What was wrong with this girl? My older sister's courtships were none of my business. And Jontan wasn't *my* friend, he was hers.

"Yeah, I'm really sad about it," I said flatly. "So why don't you leave me alone?"

This attempt at rudeness did not drive her off.

"I know how you feel," she said, tucking a strand of hair behind her ear. The room was so crowded that this gesture nearly resulted in her elbowing a couple swooping past us in a dance full of twirls. "I miss my older sister, too. I haven't seen her since she got married. She lives two days away, and that's just too long a trip now that the house magicians can't enhance stinksap anymore."

Stinksap was what we used to fuel the carriages, and it had to be enhanced to be at all efficient. That was why the death of magic had left my sisters a lifetime's travel away. I'd never considered that family members who were theoretically within reach would also be unfeasible to visit now, though.

Grandfather Doss and Grandmother Rella, Mother's parents, lived a lot further away than a two-day journey. We'd never visited them that often, but I liked them, despite the fact that they were overly proper and fussy.

The thought of never seeing them again was unbearably depressing. My shoulders drooped.

The girl seemed to take this for sympathy. "It's awful, now being the first heir. Everybody's always looking at me. I feel like everything I do reflects on my family!"

"It does," I said. "Families share status."

She looked a little hurt. "That's not comforting."

"You want comfort, or you want truth?" I asked. "Don't worry. It's not like being the first heir means much. You'll only inherit the land if your parents die soon. If they don't, you'll get married, and they'll have to adopt another heir."

"You say really uncomfortable things!" she exclaimed. "For your information, those aren't the only options! I could easily get married, my husband and I could live in the house with my parents, and they could adopt one of our children as their heir!"

And that's not an uncomfortable thing? I wondered.

You could only share status with people in your immediate family. That meant that if all your children got married, and you didn't want your status to die with you and the person you were married to, it was necessary to adopt somebody else's child to become your heir.

It was a common practice. It was also creepy.

Yeah, I knew Father had done it. That was how he had become a landowner heir, despite his parents being vassals. And Grandfather and Grandmother had been fully supportive. As far as everyone had looked at the situation, it was a business arrangement, nothing more.

But still. *Still.* The thought of having a child who legally belonged to somebody else creeped me out. Just because it could only be done voluntarily by all parties involved didn't mean it wasn't creepy.

The girl sighed wistfully. "I wish I could get married right now."

I glanced at her. "You're old enough. You're fourteen."

"I'm thirteen!" she exclaimed. "I'm not *old!*"

Right, as if fourteen was old. People usually lived until they were around fifty.

"A mathematician would call that one-ten-and-three, you know," I told her.

She stopped laughing and blinked. "Are you a mathematician?"

I got that a lot. People seemed to make that assumption when they noticed I was older than twelve and didn't have status.

"No," I said. "But I have ears."

She looked puzzled. "What do you mean?"

"I mean, mathematician numbers are so much easier than normal numbers that it's impossible to *not* memorize them once you've heard them a few times."

She gave me a blank look. "But mathematician numbers are really hard. That's why only mathematicians know how to use them."

"Are you kidding?" I exclaimed. "Mathematicians' numbers are ridiculously simple! Listen: *Ka, pe, ni, mo, du, wa, le, yi, go, bu.* There's also *zum,* for zero. They're super, super easy!"

"But normal numbers are easier than that."

"Normal numbers are tongue-twisters! *Yuluya, alalala, morova, muvava,* and *valvava!* Come on! No wonder nobody bothers to count higher than five!"

"There's nothing past five."

I rolled my eyes. Was I the only person who bothered to read older books? "There are *lots* of numbers past five. They just haven't been used much in a long time."

"Oh!" she cried. "Like counting ages!"

"No, that's a completely different numbering system. One, two, three and four are *vareshikanar, ahbarilalo, hulilibarof,* and *vwillilaroba.* It's a terrible numbering system. Every single word is five syllables that have to be memorized, and there's no pattern to them. The conversion from consecutive to ordinal to turn them into numbers for heir rankings is even worse. *Vareshikanarva, ahbarilalobof, hulilibarofoi, vwillilarobazom* . . . it's ridiculous. They all add a random extra syllable at the end for no good reason!"

"No, they make sense," she said defensively.

"Okay, what's *hwifelgarilo?*"

She was silent.

"Three-tens-and-five years old. What's *lofaliluraflor?*"

"Nobody car—"

"It's a four-tens-and-seventh heir."

"You shouldn't be using mathematician numbers!" she cried.

"Why not?" I demanded. "They're useful."

"Nobody needs those numbers!" she exclaimed. "All you need to know is one to twenty and a few of the others afterwards!"

"But if you used mathematician numbers, you wouldn't have to memorize a hundred different irregular five-syllable words to be able to know people's exact ages after a certain point, or to figure out which heir is higher ranked in a long hierarchy. It'd be easy."

"Mathematician numbers are much longer than five syllables," she said huffily. "I've heard them."

"Yeah, but they're *predictable*," I said. "You just use combinations of those same syllables. *Ka-bu-du.*" One-ten-and-five. "*Pe-bu-go.*" Two-tens-and-nine. "*Ni-bu-zum-pe.*" Three-hundreds-and-one-ten-and-two. "*Mo-bu-zum-zum-zum-zum-wa.*" Four-hundred-thousand-and-six.

She was looking peeved now. "I told you not to do that!"

"Oh, but I wasn't done," I said. "The conversion to ordinals in their numbering system makes sense: they just add *tui* to the front. And our numbering system doesn't even *have* words for multiplying or dividing."

"'Multi'— wha— huh?!"

"Mathematician words," I said smugly. "Like I said, I have ears. *Mo-foi-ka* means 'make four duplicates of this one group of things,' and *ka-hui-mo* means 'break this one group into four equal piles.'"

"Stop it!" she exclaimed, putting her hands over her ears. "Stop saying things like that! You're gonna get us —" She stopped, gulped, and looked around with a paranoid expression. Then she hissed, "You're gonna get us both killed for landowner use of mathematics!"

I rolled my eyes. Right. Like that was *really* a death crime. I knew it was in the Book of Oaths, but seriously, how could that even be enforceable?

"I'm getting up now," she announced, hopping to her feet, her skirts swishing around her. She paused and gave me a coy look. "Do you want to dance?"

"Not really," I said. "I hate dancing."

She gave me a furious look and stormed off in a huff.

A few minutes later, watching her dance with someone else, it suddenly dawned on me that she was really, really pretty.

I put my head on my knees and moaned. I really, really hated social events.

About a month later, I gobbled up the last of my dinner and looked across the table to where Mother, Father, Grandfather, and Grandmother were still working on their food.

Now seemed as good a time as any to tell them my news.

"I took the oath of mathematics," I announced casually.

Four hands paused, four spoons frozen on the way to four mouths.

"You mean you're *going* to take the oath of mathematics?" Grandfather asked finally.

"No, I've already taken the oath of mathematics. I looked it up in the Book of Oaths and I read it out loud. I did that a few days ago."

"You did *WHAT?!*" Father exploded.

"Hurik . . ." Mother looked aghast. "For one thing, you're supposed to wait for an oath ceremony . . ."

I gave her an obstinate look. "But I don't want a social event."

"For another thing, that's the sort of thing you should tell your family before you *do* it!" Father shouted.

"When did you even decide you wanted to be one?!" Mother exclaimed.

I hesitated. I could hardly say, *When a pretty girl got mad at me for talking about numbers, and I realized that the only kind of girl who'd understand me would be a girl who was a mathematician, and then I realized that I'd only understand* her *if I was one too, and . . .*

That wasn't the sort of thing you told anybody. It was way too embarrassing.

So I shrugged and said, "I dunno. When I felt like it."

Grandfather shook his head, looking exasperated. "This wasn't the way I expected you to do it."

I looked at him in surprise. "What — you thought I was going to take the oath of mathematics?"

"I did," he said calmly.

"Why?"

"Frankly? Because I thought you probably knew some already."

I grinned wryly. Apparently I wasn't the only person who could figure things out.

Mother put her face in her hands. "This is a disaster."

"No, it isn't," Grandfather said, patting her hand. "The disaster would have been if he had taken the oath of status and then gotten executed for landowner use of mathematics. I'm glad he had the good sense to choose not to do that."

"But the oath ceremony!" Mother moaned. "What will everyone think if we don't hold one?"

"Oh, we're still going to hold one," Grandmother announced, fire in her eyes. "He can take the oath again there. Nobody will be able to tell that he's already renounced status, since he never took an oath to gain it in the first place."

"Oh, come on!" I exclaimed. "I don't want an oath ceremony!"

"I'm not giving you a single other pastry until you've done one."

". . . Fine," I said sulkily.

Father shook his head in extreme displeasure, and I straightened up with a grin. Even if it meant I'd have to go through the ordeal of a pointless social event, I felt quite pleased with myself.

Now all the numbers across the Rulership were mine. And I would soon learn all of Grandfather's books' secrets.

I couldn't wait to start.

The Novice at the Rulership

"*You're* collecting the stored status?" the haughty magistrate asked scornfully, eyeing me. "You look like a child."

"I am fourteen," I said icily, dinging his status for the rudeness, "and I have a name. I'm Yaika of the Filias family, a Ruler's heir, with all the authority that entails."

He just laughed derisively.

I collected the payment silently, fuming.

Funny how four separate mathematicians, all of them extremely fussy, happened to converge upon his house a few days later to audit all of his payment records for the past year.

I have no idea who told them to do that.

The Painting like the Rulership

"You should really learn the first thing before the second," Raneh warned me.

"Yeah, yeah," I said, too excited to care about the proper order of learning her new fire magic thing. "Okay, I'm changing the colors now!"

The flames turned red, blue, purple, orange, yellow, black, green. I was able to paint an entire scene from Central, flickering in flaring light.

"It works!" I shrieked in jubilation. "It looks just like the real thing!"

I reached out to grab my new painting —

And yelped and sucked on my fingers.

My sister looked exasperated. "The first thing would be fireproofing."

Tie-ins for the

Fairy Senses

series

Fairy Feet

Daisy flipped over her medal. "Okay, the fairies are going backwards," she said. "In just a minute, it should be safe for you to run around. Just a minute..."

Maricela shifted eagerly on the front step.

Daisy watched the blue blurs zoom off. Her friend Maricela could touch fairies and not see them, which meant she could run into them, so she had to move carefully. Fortunately, Daisy could make fairies move closer to her or further away, so she made the fairies go away whenever Maricela wanted to play.

"Okay, the fairies are all gone!" Cassie reported. She giggled. "One of them was flying backwards and couldn't figure out why. She looked really annoyed."

Daisy felt a stab of jealousy. It was neat to be able to see blue blurs and move them around magnetically, but Cassie could actually *see* fairies. She was really lucky.

Maricela popped up from the stairs and jumped up and down. "Who should start?" she asked. "Who should be 'it'?"

"I'll do it," Cassie said. "On your mark... get set... go!"

With a shriek, Maricela exploded up onto the grass. She was faster, so Cassie got Daisy first. Daisy tried to catch her back, but Cassie got away.

Both Cassie and Maricela were better at running than she was. After a few minutes, Daisy was breathing heavily.

"I need to sit on the steps," she panted. "You two keep playing."

"Okay," Cassie said, pushing her glasses up her nose. She was breathing heavily, too, but she didn't look as tired as Daisy.

Maricela didn't look tired at all.

Daisy watched them running around. She glanced around the yard. At the very edge, there were some blue blurs flying. They must be out of range of her magnet. One of them flew straight at Maricela, who was racing straight at it.

"Watch out!" Daisy screamed.

The two smashed into each other, and the blue blur fell to the ground. Daisy gasped and flipped her medal over, then raced over to where Maricela was picking up the fairy, looking very concerned.

"Did I hurt the fairy?" she asked, looking like she was about to cry. "I thought it was safe!"

"It's my fault," Daisy said, biting her lip. "The yard's too big. I should've stayed in the middle."

"You couldn't have known," Cassie said, kneeling down. "We didn't measure how far your medal pushes fairies away."

Daisy touched her medal guiltily.

Cassie leaned forward to look at the blue blur, and she sighed with relief. "He's all right," she reported. "He's rubbing his head, and he looks scared, but I don't think he's hurt."

"What does he look like?" Daisy asked wistfully.

"He has wings like rows of corn, blobby and yellow. His skin's lighter than mine, but it's darker than yours," Cassie said. "Oh, he's missing a shoe."

Maricela felt around in the grass with her free hand. She picked up something invisible and twisted it around the bottom of the blue blur.

"Now it's on," Cassie said.

"I'm sorry," Maricela said to the blue blur. "I didn't mean to run into you. We were just trying to play tag."

A blue blur flashed across the yard. Daisy jerked back, startled. There was a fairy flying at them, moving much faster than fairies usually did.

"You'd better dodge," Cassie said with alarm. "There's a fairy flying really, really —"

The blue blur leapt up from Maricela's hands and moved around rapidly. The fast-moving blur dodged to the side and kept on going without hitting Maricela. In a minute, the second blue blur was gone.

"What did he do?" Daisy asked in amazement.

"He moved his hands and his mouth," Cassie said. "I think he was shouting a warning."

"That was nice of him," Maricela said. She felt around for a moment, and then patted the blue blur on the head.

The blue blur twisted away, then floated up to Maricela's head. It settled on top of her hair, right near her forehead. Something moved back and forth.

"Stop kicking me," Maricela grumbled, putting her hand up to her forehead. "Your feet are really big."

"Maybe this would work even better," Cassie said slowly. "Maybe, instead of driving all the fairies away, he could sit on your head and warn them."

Maricela's eyes widened. "Do you think that would work?"

"Let's try!" Daisy said. "We'll find out!"

They all scrambled up to their feet.

"I'll be 'it' this time," Maricela said, her eyes sparkling. "Ready . . . set . . ."

Daisy shrieked and jumped to her feet. Cassie followed quickly. Maricela raced after both of them.

A blue blur was flying straight at her, but then it dodged. That happened again a minute later. Then again.

"It's working!" Daisy cried, pausing to point at two that had avoided Maricela at once.

Maricela caught her, and smacked a hand right into her back. "Tag! You're 'it'!"

Daisy pouted. *No fair using fairies as distractions.*

"I think the fairy's having fun riding you," Cassie called from across the yard. "He's got a big grin on his face."

Maricela turned and grinned, too.

Daisy grabbed that split second to smack her arm, shout "Tag!" and then run away.

Fairy Fingers

"Hey!" Sunflower yelped, leaping to the side.

Her brother looked up from his homework. "What?"

"Not you," Sunflower fumed. "An aerial anthropoid apparently decided it would be enticing recreation to prod me with a manual protrusion in order to observe how I would react."

"Yeah, the fairies poke me too," Davis said. "Ignore it."

Sunflower most certainly would not ignore it! She got out her thesaurus to start looking for creative insults to call the multitudinously vexatious fairies —

And then she noticed that her brother was spinning his finger around, grinning slyly.

"HEY!" Sunflower shouted. "Stop sending them my way!"

Fairy Stink

"Bianca told me a secret," Jasmine said, holding her nose. There was a fairy with stinky feet sitting on Maricela's head. "But I can't tell you what it is. I wish I could. It's really, *really* funny."

"Is it the story of her brother doing his laundry wrong, so now his underwear is all pink?"

Jasmine gaped. "What?! How did you know?!"

"Bianca told me."

Jasmine was furious. Then Bianca had just been testing her? Grrr!

"Come on," she said, grabbing Maricela's hand.

"Huh? Where are we going?"

"You're going to put a fairy with stinky feet on Bianca's head."

Tie-ins for the

Dragon Eggs

series

Dragon's Dawn

Rose unlocked and turned the handle of the empty laboratory where they had been permitted to store their child. In a box in the corner, a *Deinonychus antirrhopus* egg was snuggled with a blanket, warm and hidden from prying eyes.

"Hello, Virgil," Rose said, walking over. She sat down beside the egg and brushed aside the absurd teddy bear her husband-to-be had brought for him. According to Henry, a child should have a toy to cuddle with. According to Rose, the child was currently inside an egg.

She felt a stirring in her mind, a sensation she was gradually becoming more used to. *Deinonychus* dragons were, they had discovered, telepathic. This was good, because there was no way they could have communicated with the fetus otherwise, nor even known that he was intelligent.

"Are you asleep now?" Rose asked.

Warmth. Comfort. Sleepiness. Gone.

Rose reached into the bag she had brought with her and removed her textbook and notebook. Carefully, she smoothed down the pages and began taking notes. She had splurged and spent the five cents on the subway because she had a great deal of studying to do before next week, and she had not wanted to spend an extra hour walking. Quiet would suit her perfectly.

Try as she might, though, she could not ignore the fact that her wedding was tomorrow. Her wedding to a man who was still little more than a stranger, in order to parent a child who was not even their species. Her mind skittered away from the notes she was taking, and terror squeezed her heart.

What am I doing? Rose thought frantically. Her fingers tightened around the edge of her notebook. *Almost all of the women in college are single. I know no women with a baby and a career. I'm determined to become a paleontologist, which is a difficult field to break into in any case. Am I destroying my whole future?*

Her fingers tightened around the notebook, crumpling the paper.

And then there's Henry. What if I'm wrong about him? What if he becomes chauvinistic once we're married, like my father? He's already shown signs of inflexibility!

Her fingernails dug into the paper, opening a tear. Heedless, her thoughts kept on spinning into further and further fear.

And then there's Virgil! We haven't told the city that he exists yet. How will they react when they learn that not all dragons apparently died millions of years ago? He'll be seen as a miracle. He'll be seen as a monster. He'll be seen as a pet, or animal, or source for curiosity. How will we make people understand he is a person?

She wanted to cry. Her shoulders heaved.

The equivalent of a matching howl came from the egg. He was tight and he was uncomfortable and his tail was squashed and his toes were squished and he couldn't move and he hated it! He hated it, he hated it, he hated it!

Rose was in no mood to put up with a tantrum. She slammed her notebook shut.

"You're going to hatch soon," she told him sternly. "You'll be fine."

He didn't want to hatch, he wanted to stay right here, where he was warm, and comfortable, and SQUISHED! He hated it! He didn't want to be squished anymore! SQUISHED SQUISHED SQUISHED SQUISHED!

"*You* were the one who told us you were close to hatching. *You* were the one who looked forward to it eagerly. Remember?"

Nooooo! He didn't want to, he didn't want to! He was going to kick the side of the egg!

Whump. Whump. Whump. Rose could actually see the egg moving.

"If you do that, you're going to hatch right now," Rose said dryly.

The dragon sent out a burst of terror and a kaleidoscope of panic. He didn't want to hatch! He didn't have to! He would just stay here forever!

The doorknob unlocked and turned, and Henry walked in.

"Perfect timing," Rose said. "Virgil's throwing a fit. He says he doesn't want to hatch."

Whump! Whump! Whump! Whump!

"Whoa," Henry said, walking over and putting his hand on top of the leathery egg. "No one's going to force you to do anything before you're ready, Virgil. You don't have to feel rushed. You can do things at your own pace."

The egg stopped moving. The panic stilled.

Virgil's father was nice. Virgil liked his father better today.

"Thank you," Rose said with annoyance.

Virgil's mother was scared, too. She had woken him up. Virgil hadn't liked that. He'd share his memory of it.

Rose winced as her own emotions from moments before flooded back over her again, this time filtered through the dragon's perception. Henry raised his eyebrows at her.

"You're having second thoughts about the wedding?" he asked.

Rose hesitated. It wouldn't be much use to deny it, given that their son apparently could tattle on her. "Not so much second thoughts as ... doubts. Fears."

"Ah." Henry sat down beside her and tucked the teddy bear back in with the egg. That ludicrous teddy bear. "Well, I'll tell you the same thing I told to Virgil. I'm not going to force you to do anything before you're ready. If you want to wait, we can wait."

Rose drew in a deep breath. "But we have to get married as soon as possible. We've paid for the apartment. I've moved most of my clothing there. My roommates have found someone to replace me. We can't possibly delay it."

"We most certainly can, if you want to," Henry said. "We'll find a way." He made a face. "Even if your father makes my life miserable for it."

Rose laughed. Her father was a difficult man even when he liked a person, and he wasn't fond of Henry.

"I mean it," Henry said seriously. "I don't want to start a marriage with you having second thoughts. If you want to delay, we can delay."

Rose gave that serious thought. Did she want to delay?

Henry had promised not to stand in the way of her dreams, despite the fact that her ambitions were unusual for her gender. He had always treated her with respect. He was undoubtedly a better father than she was a mother. In many ways, he was the ideal match, and Virgil was a better child than she deserved.

The timing might be rushed, and that was frightening. But this was the right family.

Rose reached out to put her hand on top of Henry's.

"No," she said softly. "Tomorrow. Tomorrow will be fine."

It no longer seemed like a source of fear.

Dragon's Yowl

Henry awoke to a telepathic yowl.

He rolled over and looked down to see their dragon son, the culprit, lying on the floor beside their bed and emanating piteousness. He had apparently escaped the bathroom, where he was supposed to sleep.

Virgil had had a bad dream! He wanted to sleep with his father and mother tonight!

Henry's wife muttered, "No. The bed is flammable. You know that. Go back to your bathtub, Virgil."

But Virgil was lonely! Virgil was sad! Virgil had had a bad dream!

And that was how Henry ended up sleeping in the bathtub that night.

Tie-ins for the Trilogy of a Teenage Werevulture series

Trials of a Teenage Shapeshifter

Some people are werewolves. They're lucky. They can put on collars with tags and go outside during the full moon.

Some people are werebears. They've got it good. They can pig out on human food, and no one bothers a bear in the woods.

Some people are wererats. That's decent. As long as they don't go outside, they're perfectly fine.

Some people are werecats. They have the best of all worlds.

I'm not a werewolf.

I'm not a werebear.

I'm not a wererat.

I'm not a werecat.

I'm a werevulture.

And boy, does our next door neighbor's garbage look good.

Triumph of a Teenage Werevulture

A ten-foot-tall Mosquito smashed into a Weretick, and a pileup ensued.

Our school and the rival school had the worst names in football team history. And I still didn't know how I'd gotten roped into going.

The faun beside me pumped his fists in the air and cheered. He hadn't even looked at me since the game had started.

I sighed and pulled out my phone. When Jerry Basajaunclanfaun had asked me to Homecoming, I'd assumed he meant the dance. It turned out he'd meant the game. When I'd asked him an hour ago about what color of tux he was wearing to the dance, he had given me a blank look.

Worst. Date. Ever.

I can't believe I bought a dress and everything, I texted Kegan furiously. I'd been complaining for the past hour.

You can come with me and Donald if Jerry's not going to take you, Kegan typed.

Donald wouldn't like that, I said.

If Donald doesn't like it, then I'll dump him!!!!! Kegan informed me.

I grinned. I had a great best friend. But still, tagging along on her date wouldn't be any fun. *Nah, it's fine*, I wrote.

My eyes wandered to the field, where a cyclops caught a ball intended for a satyr, then an abarimon stole the ball from him and took off running. Despite the fact that abarimons had backwards feet, they ran surprisingly fast. Even without using their magical ability to run at supersonic speeds.

See, that was the reason I didn't like football. It was just so boring. All the other sports allowed magic, or at least shifting. In baseball, watching specters turn insubstantial to keep from getting tagged out when the ball was thrown at them was hilarious. I'd had a massive crush on a werekangaroo basketball player in junior high school, and an even bigger crush on a wereseagull baseball player last year. And golf, well, nothing could make golf interesting, but the way duergars made their balls burrow underground instead of flying through the air was sort of cool.

But football banned anything except for physical abilities. No magic, no shifting, no insubstantiality, no nothing. Like, seriously, who found this sport interesting?

"Wooooooooo!" Jerry screamed from beside me.

My date, I thought grumpily.

My phone chirped, and I glanced down. Another message from Kegan had appeared.

DEREK GIANTCLANBLEMMYES BROKE UP WITH HIS GIRLFRIEND YESTERDAY! THAT MEANS HE WON'T HAVE A DATE FOR HOMECOMING! MAYBE YOU COULD ASK HIM TO GO WITH YOU!

WHO'S THAT? I asked.

THE QUARTERBACK? HE SHOULD BE PLAYING RIGHT NOW!

I glanced up from my phone and looked down at the field. It was easy to spot the only headless football player on the field. Instead of a helmet, he had a transparent plastic dome attached to the middle of his shirt.

HE'S GOT NO HEAD, I typed. AND HIS FACE IS ON HIS CHEST.

DUH, HE'S A BLEMMYES.

SORTA MY POINT, I said.

Everybody started screaming around me. I shifted to my half-form and crammed the tops of my wings into my ears to mute out as much as possible.

DO YOU KNOW THAT HALF THE PLAYERS IN THE FOOTBALL HALL OF FAME ARE BLEMMYES? Kegan asked.

NO, I typed, bored. SO?

MY DAD SAYS IT'S IMPOSSIBLE FOR THEM TO GET BRAIN DAMAGE, SO THEY TAKE RISKS NO ONE ELSE WOULD. MY AUNT SAYS BLEMMYES ARE HOT.

I rolled my eyes. GOOD FOR HER. I LIKE GUYS WHO HAVE FACES ON THEIR HEADS.

AND WINGS? Kegan asked with a smiley face.

I scowled. I'd asked two different werebirds to Homecoming, and they'd both said no. Alec had looked really superior about it, and Manuel had said he had a date already. In the end, I'd ended up with Jerry, who had goat legs and no wings and who was completely ignoring me.

MOM COMING UP STAIRS GOTTAGOBYE a new message appeared.

I moaned and flicked off the screen of my phone. Kegan hadn't even started her homework yet, which meant her mom would be on her case until she got it done. That left me with nothing to do except watch the game.

"Hey, disappear those, wouldya?" a guy asked, tapping my shoulder. "I can't see."

I wasn't sure why he would want to see, but I shifted back to human, feeling the weird sensation of feathers slurping back into skin and skin melting into a bulge on my back.

"Yeah, Mosquitoes!" Jerry called from beside me, his face lit up with excitement.

I couldn't take this any longer. It was cruel and unusual punishment. That was against the law, wasn't it? I *had* to get up and leave.

I stood up with determination.

"Where are you going?" my date asked, glancing over at me.

"To the bathroom," I said. It was true. Never mind that I would call my dad to pick me up early and send Jerry a text saying I had gone home after that. He clearly wasn't intending to take me to the dance, which meant this was a total waste of time, and I was bored out of my skull.

"Come back quickly," he said, pointing at the field. "You don't want to miss this. Ohh! Foul!"

I agree. Foul date, I thought, edging my way through the narrow space between people's knees and the bleacher in front of us. I finally got to the steps down the middle and headed downwards. I glanced over at the bleachers on the other side of the field, seeing a woman with brown skin and a cloud of black hair. As I watched, she used the talon from a large bird foot to open a soda can.

I stopped abruptly. *Collette?*

What in the world was my older sister doing here? And sitting on the bleachers with fans of the enemy team?

Collette was in college now. She had no reason to be showing up at a high school football game. Sure, my school was her alma mater, but then why was she sitting on the other side?

I stopped at the bathroom just long enough to make my excuse true, and then headed towards my sister. I walked up the stairs and tried to squeeze past an enormous minotaur at the end, but he took one look at the crimson shirt and grey pants my date had insisted I wear, then folded his arms and glared at me, refusing to budge.

Fine, I thought, annoyed. I walked up the stairs to the top of the bleachers, ignoring all the black-and-purple-wearing fans below me. I shrank to bird form — which wasn't really that much smaller, because griffon vultures were enormous — and leapt upwards, flapping my arms, using my altitude to soar downwards to my sister's position.

She yelped as I landed, and her hand holding the soda jerked upward. The cup went flying, the specter behind her went insubstantial, the soda splashed onto the kikimora behind him instead. She gave my sister an evil glare.

Collette was too busy glaring at me to notice. "What do you think you're doing? That was so rude!"

I rustled my wings, which had caught a few drops of the flying soda, and shifted to human. The stickiness wound up on the right side of my back.

"Whatcha doing?" I asked. I glanced down at her outfit, which was purple. "And why are you wearing the enemy colors?"

"Camouflage," Collette said coolly, folding her arms.

"It's not school spirit to root for the other team," I informed her.

"I graduated. I can root for whoever I want. Besides, I'm definitely not rooting for this one." She added under her breath, "Rotten, lousy cheater . . ."

I stiffened. The other team was cheating? How? What were they doing? Why hadn't anybody stopped them?

I hadn't been watching the game much, but surely Jerry and the other nutjobs in the crowd who liked this sport would have noticed by now. Not to mention the coaches or referee or whatever.

Wouldn't they?

My sister was a werehawk. She had magically enhanced vision. She might very well have noticed things nobody else would.

I glanced at the football field. A furry guy leapt up and seized the ball.

"Is it him?" I asked immediately, pointing. "Is he, like, a werehare who has hare legs in half-form and no one knows it? Shifting on the field is forbidden, right?"

Collette ignored me.

A player threw the ball halfway across the field, where it went through something tall like a two-pronged fork and a lot of people cheered.

"Did someone help the ball go that far?" I asked. "A vila? They control wind. Or a poltergeist? They have telekinesis."

"Shut up," Collette muttered, looking annoyed.

My imagination went into overdrive. This was much more interesting than watching the game played correctly, so I watched with silent excitement for several minutes, thinking about all of the possibilities.

All abatwas could shrink really tiny. Maybe a tomte had crawled inside the football and was shifting his weight around to make the ball move where he wanted.

Dryads could control water. Maybe the football was secretly full of water instead of whatever normal stuffing was supposed to be in it.

Rakshasas had illusion magic. Maybe one of them was making the ball look like it was going places it wasn't going in order to score goals.

The enemy team's cheerleaders bounced up and down, waving their pompoms and shouting one of their cheers. "Fight, fight! Feel our bite! We will make you bleed with blight! Goooooo, Wereticks!"

The cheerleaders from my school looked annoyed, and they grabbed their pompoms to start on their next cheer. The largest one, an ogre, leaned over as two tiny goblins hopped onto her arms. The ogre flung them both into the air, one at a time. They grew full-sized as they reached the top of their arcs, then shrank tiny again as they fell so that the ogre could catch them and throw them again. At the top of each arc, they shouted a letter.

"M!"
"O!"
"S!"
"Q!"
"U!"
"I!"

"T!"

"O!"

"S!"

"GOOOOOOOO, MOSQUITOES!"

"Did they misspell 'Mosquitoes'?" I asked Collette.

She shrugged, her lips pursed as she watched the enemy cheerleaders, who were climbing into a pyramid for a response. The bigger cheerleaders went at the bottom: a troll and a yeti and a tengu. A rakshasa and a poohka climbed up for the middle, and a tiny pixie flew to the top.

They waved their pompoms in unison, shouting, "Watch us win! It's a breeze! We will give you Lyme disease! Gooooooooo, Wereticks!"

"First bleeding, now disease," I said. "These cheers are kind of disgusting."

The red-and-grey cheerleaders on my school's side looked indignant. They leapt up and got into a new formation. A poohka flipped upside down into the air, which seemed to me to be unwise while wearing such a short skirt, and she landed insubstantially inside the ogre.

The ogre roared the next cheer while the poohka waved insubstantial pompoms from inside her, making it look like the ogre had four arms.

"Your bite's bad! Our bite's worse! You will itch to break our curse!"

"Did they just call our football team a curse?" I asked.

The enemy cheerleading squad's rakshasa waved her hand, and all of their clothes changed colors in a rainbow whirl. Now they were wearing red and grey, and had big mosquito wings on their backs. The girls pranced into a line and twisted their fists in front of their eyes.

"Oh, boo hoo! We're so lame! Wereticks beat us every game!"

Wow. This was starting to get really personal.

I glanced over at my sister. She was watching the enemy side's cheerleaders, with no sign of looking across the field again. I realized that she hadn't looked at our side's cheerleaders once during the increasingly aggressive exchange.

Aha! I realized. "Is one of them the cheater?"

"Yes," Collette muttered.

"Which one?" I asked eagerly.

Collette said nothing.

The rakshasa? I thought. *With her power, she'd be able to — oh, but wait, Collette's not glaring at her. She's glaring at . . .*

"The troll?" I asked.

Collette let out an incoherent growl.

The troll cheerleader was eight feet tall and had a face like the back of a bus.

"She looks like she should be playing football, not cheering for it," I commented.

"I know, right?" Collette said huffily.

No wonder the cheerleader was sabotaging the game. She was probably mad that she wasn't allowed to play because the school had no girls' football team. Except, how? Aside from growing taller when they wanted to, like all giants could, trolls had no magical abilities.

"Is somebody helping her cheat?" I asked.

"Obviously!" Collette snapped.

I pondered all through the Mosquito cheerleaders' retaliation, which attacked the Wereticks' costumes, and then the comeback from the Wereticks, which insulted the Mosquitoes' head cheerleader. This was getting unreal.

"If she's cheating, somebody should stop her," I said at last.

Collette snorted.

"Aren't you going to?" I asked.

"Mind your own beeswax," Collette snapped.

Okay. If my sister wasn't going to do anything about it, and I was the only other person who knew about the cheating, that meant it was my duty. I reached for the bird inside and shrank down to vulture.

Collette turned and eyed me suspiciously. "What are you —"

I leapt into the air, spread my wings, and swooped down toward the enemy cheerleaders, shrieking like a garbage truck at war with an enraged dinosaur.

The cheerleaders screamed and scattered, and I somehow managed to maintain enough control to veer after the troll.

She screamed and punched me.

I flipped over backwards, toppled to the ground, and lay there, stunned and in pain.

I ignored the whistle and yells of "Foul!"

There was a piercing, high-pitched cry, and a hawk landed beside me. She shifted into my older sister, garbled hawk shrieks turning into human shouting as her face changed from beak to mouth.

"— in the world did you think you were doing?! You idiot!"

"You weren't planning to do anything!" I shouted. "Somebody had to stop the troll from cheating and messing up the game!"

"The *game?*" Collette yelled. "You think this was about the *game?*"

I stood up and clutched my side. Ow ow ow. It felt like I had a nasty bruise there. That troll cheerleader punched hard. "Yeah . . . ?"

"Hello!" Collette shouted. "When I said she was cheating, I meant with my *boyfriend!*" She glared at the troll and pointed an accusing finger at her.

The troll gulped and hid behind the yeti. I'd never seen a troll blush before.

"Your . . . boyfriend," I repeated slowly.

"Don't try to deny it!" Collette snapped, giving the troll cheerleader a hostile glare.

The troll shrunk to a normal five-foot-five height, fidgeting with her hands while still hiding behind the yeti. "Well . . . I mean . . . I mean, he used to be my boyfriend, and we only broke up because he went to college, and all I did was say I wanted him back . . ."

"Oh, for crying out loud, you think this is worth interrupting the game?" the rakshasa cheerleader asked sarcastically, stepping forward.

"You got a problem with that?" Collette shouted.

"Bite me!" the rakshasa snapped.

"Bite me, too!" I yelled, siding with my sister.

The rakshasa bared her teeth to reveal two wickedly curved vampire fangs.

"Changed my mind," I said quickly.

A pair of paramedics arrived. One of them, a dracula, sliced his fingertip and squeezed a few drops of blood into a paper cup and handed it to me. His fingertip healed instantly.

Urrrrrrrgh. Vampire blood tasted disgusting. But I was too sore to protest. I took the cup and let the drops trickle into my mouth, shuddering at the nasty taste that seemed to cloy all the way down my throat.

But that wasn't the last of it. Oh no. The two schools' coaches marched over: an ogre who was currently twelve feet tall and a djinn who was blasting fire around him in fury.

"Well, on the bright side," I said philosophically, sitting in the car next to my sister, "we have a lifetime ban from ever attending the school's football games again."

"Goody," she said sourly, twisting her key in the ignition.

"Do you want to talk about it?" I asked.

Collette slammed her fist against the steering wheel several times, and then stopped and breathed deeply.

"No," she said at last. "If Jason was cheating, it's good riddance anyway. It's just, *argh*."

"He was hot," I nodded.

"And I don't know why he decided to cheat on me!"

"It's obvious," I told her. "He prefers ugly girls to pretty ones. You never had a chance."

A smirk played across Collette's lips. "That's possible."

"Hey, can we ditch the car and fly home?" I asked hopefully. "I've got my learner's permit now, and since you have a flyer's license —"

"Forget it," Collette snorted, letting go of the brake and backing out of our parking space. "The last time we flew together, you crashed into a dracula."

"That was his fault!" I said defensively. "Bats aren't supposed to be out in midday, so I wasn't expecting —"

"*No*," she said.

My phone chirped, and I tugged it out of my pocket. To my surprise, there was a text from Jerry.

2 COOL ATTACKING CHEERLEADER! PICK U UP AT 8?

"Who was it?" Collette asked.

"My date." I grinned. "I'm going to Homecoming tomorrow."

This game might just have been worth it, after all.

Trials of a Teenage Zombie

"How's Collette's birthday party going?" Kegan asked me over the phone.

I shrugged. "Surreal. Her friends from college have weird tastes."

"Like what?"

"Well, the vegetarian minotaur keeps complaining about the dead cow we're serving for refreshments, the sasquatch keeps trying to groom me, and a zombie and a werefalcon are fighting over who gets to eat the last bite."

"Of what?"

I put the phone on speaker so she could hear.

"It's my brain!" the zombie shouted.

"No, MY brain!" the falcon yelled.

I shook my head in exasperation. "See? Everybody knows the heart and lungs are much yummier."

Tie-ins for THE NUMBERS JUST KEEP GETTING BIGGER series

ONE SILLY CHATTERBOX THAT WON'T STOP TALKING

"What are you doing?" I chirped, ducking into the house of our newest neighbor. "I hear you're a scribe! Do you work for Josefa? He's the bookbinder who lives down the street. My name's Henina. I'm six years old. Did you hear the prophecy this morning?"

The man at the desk turned around. His eyes were squinty in the dim gloom, and his fingers looked cramped. He shook them out slowly while he talked. "No, I'm afraid I didn't. I was busy working."

"It was funny!" I declared. "The prophecy said that there would be hiccupping all through the land, and as soon as all the soothsayers and fortune tellers finished, everyone started to hiccup! Really loudly! Me, too!"

"That would explain why I caught the hiccups this morning," the man said dryly. "I've no doubt that every person in the kingdom did at the same time."

I giggled. "The Fates are sometimes funny."

"They are." He nodded. "It's a bit concerning."

"Why?" I cocked my head to the side.

"Because I'm not sure they consider us any more than entertainment . . . ah, but never mind. I'm working on a treatise about the qualities of the Fates, so they're on my mind. Are you Josefa's daughter?"

"No!" I laughed. "My father's Dar. He told me to leave the house because I kept breaking the things he was trying to fix. I wasn't really breaking them, though — I was just taking them apart, and he didn't believe me when I said I could remember how to put them back together. What're you doing?"

"I'm copying over this page," he said. "When I'm done writing it, I'll add some illustrations to make it beautiful. This is a book for a noble family, so the quality has to be top-notch."

"Can I help?" I asked hopefully. "I'm good at drawing. I practice on the walls a lot with ash from the stove. Ma gets mad."

"Ah . . . ha ha." He laughed awkwardly. "Ink and paper is a little different from that."

"I can learn," I said. "I'm a fast learner."

"I'm sure you are." He coughed. "But you need to understand how expensive paper is, and how important it is not to waste it."

I frowned. "How much is it?"

"An iron for every page."

I yelped. "An *iron*? For every *page*?"

"That's right."

"But you can buy four apples for that! Five, if you get wormy ones!"

"I told you it's expensive."

"That means a three-hundred-page book would cost eighteen coppers and twelve irons!"

The scribe looked startled. "That's . . . right. How did you figure that out so quickly?"

"Because that's how much it is!"

"Well . . . technically that's not the cost of a book," he said. "Even if all you want is a book of empty pages, you will have to pay to have the pages sewn up and the wooden covers attached, which is an additional tin."

"A tin?! That brings the total to three tins, five coppers, and four irons!"

"Yes. And that's only for a blank book. The cost for having a scribe write the text in is at least a silver. With illustrations, it can be much higher. The cost for the manuscript I'm working on currently, for example, was one silver, five tins, and four coppers."

"WHAT!" I screamed.

"Yes. So you can see why I cannot afford to let you help me."

"That's the same as three thousand, six hundred and forty-eight irons!" I yelled.

He blinked. "How do you know that?"

"Sixteen irons to a copper, eight coppers to a tin, twelve tins to a silver, twenty-four silvers to a gold," I said. "Everybody knows that."

He frowned. "Yes, but . . . you're six years old."

"So?"

"So, even most *adults* aren't that fast at calculating the conversions between any coins except coppers and irons."

I shrugged. "It's money. I like money."

"Or you're a very smart child," he said, eyeing me thoughtfully.

I grinned. "Can you tell Pa that? He told me taking apart all of the things he had been hired to fix was stupid."

"You know, when I was your age, my parents made great sacrifices to pay a tutor to teach me how to read," the scribe said slowly. "They felt it was worth it because I was smart. With your intelligence, I think you could learn, as well. Then you would have the option to work as a scribe, or perhaps a tutor for a noble family. Both of those jobs would pay well enough that you would never need to worry about going hungry."

"Could I get a dog?" I asked hopefully.

"Probably not. Only rich families can afford to have pets."

"Then I want to be rich," I informed him.

He laughed. "So do we all."

"Can *you* teach me?" I asked.

He paused. "I suppose it's possible, but that wasn't what I was suggesting. It would be better to go to an actual teacher. In any case, you'd have to ask your parents, as teaching a child to read takes a great deal of time, so it would cost a lot of money."

"What if it didn't take *any* time?" I asked shrewdly.

He laughed. "I'm afraid that's a bit optimistic."

"I already know the basics!" I said. "The bookbinder taught me!"

The scribe paused. "Josefa did?"

"Uh huh." I nodded. "I kept pestering him until he did. He said I was a silly chatterbox that never stopped talking, and if I'd leave him alone for an hour, he'd teach me one thing that took him two minutes. He taught me all the basics that way."

"I can easily see that," our new neighbor said dryly.

"So, what if I teach myself the rest?" I said excitedly. "What if you let me read the pages while you're working on them? Then I can practice!"

The man stared at me thoughtfully. "Do you really think that's all you would need?"

"Uh huh!" I said.

"And you won't make any noise?"

ONE SILLY CHATTERBOX THAT WON'T STOP TALKING

"Umm, that I can't promise."

"I *do* need to be able to concentrate," he said sternly. "That's why I keep the windows closed, so I don't have to hear noise from outside."

I was alarmed. "I can be helpful! I can read all the pages you make and the pages you copy from and make sure they're always the same!"

"That . . . um . . . hmm." He paused. "That could be helpful, actually. But it would require you to read both very carefully. Are you sure you can do that?"

"I'm sure I can try!" I said confidently.

He started to laugh. Then he got up and walked out of the room, coming back with a beat-up old chair under his arm from the kitchen. He set it beside the chair he'd been sitting on.

"You can't touch the pages," he warned, "but you can read over my shoulder. Let's see if you can teach yourself how to read."

THREE LITTLE STONES THAT SAID THE WRONG THING

"You shouldn't be doing this," Darson griped. "Marrying a total stranger!"

"*You're* the one who should be doing this," Elayn sniffed.

"I'm not gonna marry a total stranger!" Darson yelled.

"Then find somebody you know!" Elayn yelled back. "You're not gonna be ineligible for the draft until you're married and have a kid!"

My oldest brother and sister's argument was so loud that I couldn't hear myself think, which wasn't hard because I always thought by talking out loud, so I wandered down the hall to get to the bedroom that I shared with all three of my sisters.

Inside the bedroom, Carran was getting ready, tying on what had been Elayn's best dress the day before yesterday.

Seeing me come in, she giggled. "This is so romantic!"

"It's not romantic," I grumbled, pulling the loose swathes of fabric back onto my shoulders. "It's dumb because Elayn could have picked someone herself instead of saying that she wants to let the Fates decide for her. She could have picked any young man she knows. She's pretty, and none of them want to be drafted. And it's not fair that I have to wear your old dress. It's too baggy, and it's itchy!"

"You're only eight," Carran said knowingly. "When you're twelve, like me, you'll understand that it's far more romantic for Elayn to do things this way."

"So what you're saying is, I'll become stupid?"

"And the dress isn't *that* itchy!"

"It feels like you deliberately put fleas in it."

"Maaaaaaa!" Carran yelled. "Henina's being rude!"

"So what else is new?" Ma called from down the hallway.

"Make her stop!"

"Would that I could!"

I smirked.

"You don't understand anything," Carran told me huffily. "Things always work out best if you leave them up to the Fates."

"No, things always happen if the Fates say they're going to. There's a difference."

"You don't understand anything," Carran told me huffily. "Elayn is doing this to save a young man from the draft. Assuming she gets pregnant right away, he'll be ineligible by this time next year."

"Yes, a stranger she's never met! Why does she *care*?"

"It's *altruism*," Carran informed me. She stared off into space with starry eyes. "The Fates will make sure she ends up with the right man."

"You mean like the way the Fates made sure it didn't rain in the market last month because they'd prophesied it wouldn't?"

"He'll be the perfect young man for her. After the matching today, they'll get married in one week —"

"I mean, I'll admit it was really funny when all those bedsheets that were hanging out to dry zoomed up in the air and the wind kept them flying around for two hours straight right underneath the cloud that was pouring above the market and then 'accidentally' wringing themselves out off in the streets, so the market didn't get wet. That was hilarious."

"— and it'll be the most beautiful —"

"Do you think the Fates will make Elayn's perfect man zoom through the air, like those bedsheets? That would be entertaining. I wouldn't mind going to the ceremony if we get to see that."

"— thing ever, because the Fates will reward Elayn for her self-sacrificing nobility —"

"I wouldn't mind seeing Elayn fly through the air," I chattered excitedly. "Do you think the Fates will do that? Of course, that would only be funny as long as she didn't get hurt, which she might, because all those bedsheets fell to the ground with a splat when the rain was over, and I think that might be painful. I've never fallen that far, but it looked uncomfortable. I'm glad I'm not a bedsheet."

"Maaaaaaa!" Carran complained. "Henina won't stop talking!"

"So what else is new?" Ma called back.

"Of course, if I *were* a bedsheet, that would mean the Fates might make me fly, which would be fun to experience . . ." I mused.

In a huff, Carran stalked out of the room.

I was still talking about flying bedsheets when we left to walk to the market in the middle of the city, which was where the matching ceremony was to be held, but that was okay because nobody was listening to me, so I could think out loud in peace. Except for the nine times Orran told me to shut up, anyway.

The whole way there, Elayn and Darson kept on arguing over whether this was a good idea, which was a silly argument, because obviously it wasn't. But when I started thinking about that, Pa and Adarr got mad at me for "taking sides."

"I wasn't taking sides, I was just thinking," I objected.

"Then think silently!" Pa said.

I tried, but I got yelled at several more times before I changed the subject and started thinking about something else instead.

We arrived at the market at the same time as a lot of young men and women and their families.

"It's more crowded than usual, even though the stalls are all closed," I noticed. "That's weird. If I sold things, I'd want to be here to sell to everyone."

"Yes, so do the sellers," Pa said. "But when the king used to allow it, it made everything such chaos that he put his foot down and said they can't sell during matching ceremonies anymore."

"Then why do people bring their money with them?" I asked.

"Who knows?" Pa shrugged. He paused. "What makes you say people brought their money?"

"Because that pickpocket right there is very busy." I pointed.

Pa put a hand to his pocket, looking panicked.

"Elayn!" a semi-familiar voice said.

I looked over, and saw Elayn and Darson's argument was being interrupted by a young man I vaguely knew.

"Oh, he lives in our neighborhood," I noted, figuring out why. "Or rather, a few streets away. His father carves wood. He's pretty good at it."

"Kakson!" Elayn cried, her cheeks turning faintly pink. "Are you here for the matching ceremony?"

THREE LITTLE STONES THAT SAID THE WRONG THING

"My parents insisted," he said, looking embarrassed. "They want me ineligible for the draft as soon as possible. Is Darson here to be matched, too?"

"When cows rain from the sky," Darson said succinctly.

"The Fates might do that someday," I said. "They did it with bedsheets."

"No, I'm the one who's here for that." Elayn giggled, her face turning even redder. "I thought I'd leave my future in the hands of the Fates."

"Which was a terrible idea," I put in helpfully. "The Fates aren't known for being nice to people."

Kakson didn't seem to hear me. He was staring at my older sister, his mouth agape. "*You?* But — but why you?"

"Why *not* me?" Elayn raised her chin. "I can trust in the Fates just like anybody, can't I?"

"But — but —"

"But you're pretty," I finished for him. "Maybe not so bright in this particular instance, but —"

"SHUT UP!" Elayn and Kakson both yelled at me.

I decided to wander off into the crowd while everyone else in my family was absorbed in watching their conversation. Maybe then everybody would stop yelling at me.

"There sure are a lot of pickpockets around," I commented. "Oh, one of them just stole a coin from that fat woman's dress."

The rich-looking woman I was passing heard me, felt her pocket, and let out a loud scream. The man who had just picked her pocket bolted through the crowd with her chasing after him.

"She's hollering threats, but he's better at running," I noted as I kept on walking. "He's going to get away. Yep. He did."

For some reason, no one ever seemed to notice the pickpockets and cutpurses doing their work. It was always obvious to me which people were sneaking and trying to steal things.

"Why doesn't anybody ever notice them?" I wondered.

Then I stopped as something *really* weird caught my eye.

"Why did that mean-eyed rich man sneak coins *into* that woman's hand?" I murmured. "That makes no sense. She's obviously a fortune teller, so he could just pay her to read his fortune. He doesn't have to sneak. Oh, she peeked at the coins. They're tins! Why would anybody pay a fortune teller that much?"

I moved forward because the mystery was so interesting. I even tried to keep my mouth shut so that they wouldn't notice I was listening in.

". . . the prettiest girl here," the mean-eyed young man in the expensive clothes was murmuring to the fortune teller. "Got it?"

"Of course." The fortune teller's fingers curled around the coins, and she tucked them into a hidden pocket down her neckline.

Fingers grabbed my arm.

I jumped, startled, and looked around.

It was Pa.

"Henina!" he scolded. "Don't wander off! It's not safe!"

"I was just listening to —"

"No, you can't pester the fortune tellers!" he scolded, grabbing my right hand and marching me back to where the rest of the family was. "They're here to do the matching, not to deal with nosy children. They need to concentrate!"

"On what?" I asked, interested.

"Maybe if you keep your mouth shut and your eyes open, you'll be able to figure that out."

"I learn a lot more with my eyes *and* my mouth open."

He snorted. "Like what?"

"Like who the pickpockets in the crowd are. We passed by one a second ago."

Pa frantically checked his pocket. His face went white.

"It's okay," I said, unclenching my left fist and holding out the three irons that had been there. "I saw him coming and I took them out of your pocket first. You should put them in your sock instead so that nobody can steal them."

Pa took the money from me, looking a combination of exasperated and relieved.

About an hour later, after a bunch of boring speeches were said by soothsayers and Pa caught me trying to wander off again, all the young men and women who were here to be matched were moved to the center of the crowd, where they stood in an empty space so everyone could watch them.

"There are only sixteen," I told Pa. "I thought there'd be more of them. And only three of them are girls."

THREE LITTLE STONES THAT SAID THE WRONG THING

"More young men are desperate to be matched than young women," Pa told me in an undertone. "That's why it's so good of your sister to be here."

"But that means ten of the boys aren't going to be matched," I whispered back. "Also, it's not a good thing to do, it's stupid."

"Shhhh!"

Two fortune tellers were walking around the circle of young men and women, holding out a bowl full of colorful stones. They were all distinctive colors and shapes, easy to remember and hard to mistake for one another.

"It must've taken a lot of work to find all those stones in different colors," I murmured, impressed. "Colorful stones are usually more expensive. Wait, all of those are painted. Those aren't their natural colors. That's not nearly as impressive."

"Shhhh!"

I watched as everyone chose a stone. Elayn's was brilliant blue, the color of the sky on a cloudless noon. Kakson's was grey and lumpy. It looked like a deformed iron coin. The mean-eyed young man in fancy clothes chose a stone that was red and shiny.

The fortune tellers set down the large bowl they were carrying, and each of them retrieved a small box from their pocket that had a large hole in the top.

Many of the sixteen people in the circle swallowed.

The other fortune teller said, "I remind you all that, while these matches are not legally binding, they will show the will of the Fates. Refusing the will of the Fates once they have spoken is asking for misfortune to follow you. If any of you wish to depart before the matches are made, you may now do so."

I waited for Elayn to walk off.

Nobody moved.

The fortune tellers walked around the circle, collecting stones.

When the fortune teller with the young men's box got to the one with the mean eyes, he winked and feinted dropping his stone into the box while actually slipping it into her hand.

She made a slight gesture with her head off to the right.

He nodded.

The two fortune tellers walked back to their places, and the circle broke into a nervous crowd of sixteen young people all facing the same direction, watching the boxes with riveted attention.

The first two stones that came out were bright pink and lumpy, and black and skinny.

Screams of excitement came from a young man and young woman, who raced over to meet each other. There was a blabber of excitement as they tried to introduce themselves to one another at the same time, and then a crowd of other people swarmed around them, probably their families.

Once the chatter had subsided, and the first couple had moved out of the center of the crowd, the tension was thicker than ever.

The next two stones to emerge were clear and sparkly, and green-and-yellow spotted.

The young man made a desperate choking sound, and looked extremely panicked as his family had to force him to introduce himself to the young woman he'd been matched with.

"She seems insulted, probably because she thinks he doesn't want to marry her because she's ugly, but I'm pretty sure he's just really shy," I pondered, not bothering to say it quietly.

"Shut uuuuup!" Carran hissed.

Once this couple and their families had moved off into the crowd, silence fell over everyone. The fortune tellers raised their boxes.

They shook them.

My sister's stone came out of the young women's box.

The other fortune teller slipped something into the opening of her box, started to tilt it forward —

"I GET IT!" I shouted, running forward. I pointed at the rich young man. "He BRIBED her! He bribed her to make sure he got matched to the prettiest girl! That's YOU, Elayn!"

"Henina!" Elayn shrieked, looking embarrassed and furious. "What are you doing? Go back over there!"

"NO!" I ran over to the fortune teller and yanked her hand off the box. The red stone fell out.

Elayn looked down at it.

She looked up at the young man she'd been matched with.

He cleared his throat. "I promise you, there was no chicanery. It's clear this was the will of the Fates. Perhaps your sister has a talent for seeing the future —"

"No," Elayn said in a dangerous voice, "she doesn't. If she did, she would be capable of thinking things through."

"That's true," I nodded, uninsulted.

"Henina," Elayn growled, her eyebrows lowered.

"Yes?"

Her shoulders tensed. Her fists clenched.

"Thank you," she muttered.

"You're welcome!" I beamed. "See? My being unable to shut my mouth has benefits, after all! By the way, since you're already here and wanted to get matched today, you might as well pick somebody for yourself. I think you ought to choose —"

"SHUT UP!" Elayn shouted.

She stormed past the rich young man and over to Kakson.

"Well?" she demanded. "Do you want to marry me?"

"Wh-what?" He gaped at her.

She tossed her hair. "Clearly the will of the Fates would have matched us together if there hadn't been cheating."

"B-but —" He looked around frantically. "But the stones —"

"Yes, your stone, my stone, and his stone said the wrong thing," Elayn said, giving the rich young man a contemptuous look. "But that's not the will of the Fates. It was just the will of a greedy fortune teller who I won't trust again. Now, do you want to marry me or don't you?"

"Y-yes!" he gasped. "I'd love to!"

"I'm so glad I'm incapable of shutting my mouth," I beamed.

Four Hardened Criminals on a Dangerous Street

"Look at this!" I said to myself, admiring the clock I'd just found in a rich person's trash. And all I'd needed to do was go down a few dangerous streets that most people wouldn't dare walk down. Ma always told me not to go to such places, but the best prizes were in places most people didn't search. "All it needs is a few new springs, maybe new paint, and it'll be worth two tins at least!"

A ten-year-year-old boy stepped in front of me, holding a knife.

"G-give me the clock," he stammered.

"No way," I said indignantly. "This is mine. And it's only worth money if you know how to fix it. Do you?"

"Give me the clock!"

"I'll admit you chose a good street to rob somebody on," I said, "but you really ought to have a partner to make sure I can't run away. And you should be asking for the coppers in my pocket, not the trash I'm holding. I've got several, you know."

Something sharp pressed against the back of my neck. "Give me the coppers."

I sighed heavily. "I really asked for that, didn't I?"

The knife point pressed slightly harder.

"All right, all right," I muttered, leaning over to set the clock down. "Let me get them out. For crying out loud."

I reached into the hidden pocket under my armpit where I kept my money, and pulled out three of the seven coppers I had in there, careful to make sure none of the remainder showed.

I held the coins over my shoulder. They were snatched.

"Now give me the clock!" the ten-year-old boy demanded.

"I set it on the ground," I said. "If you want it, take it."

The boy set his knife on the ground and leaned over to pick up it up.

Quick as a wink, I nabbed the knife and spun around, holding its sharp edge against the back of the boy's neck while I glared at the young man who had been behind me. "Now give me my money back."

The boy let out a panicked yelp.

"Let go of him!" the young man snarled.

"No," I said amiably, holding my hand steady. "You two look alike, so I'm guessing you're brothers. You probably don't want him to die. Give me my money back."

Slowly, the young man reached into his pocket and dropped the coins on the ground. They landed with a scatter of *clinks*.

"Good try, but I'm not going to lean over to pick them up," I said. "Drop the knife, back away with your hands up, and I'll have your brother pick the coins up. Then I'll keep him as a hostage until we're within view of a guard station. At that point, I'll have him give me back my clock and let him go free. I'm keeping the knife, though. Clearly you can't be trusted with such things."

I felt a third knife prick the middle of my back. A high-pitched little girl's voice squeaked, "Let go of my brother!"

I groaned. "How young are you criminals starting these days?"

"As young as we need to!" the little girl snapped. "Pa got drafted, and Ma can't work because she's too sick, and we've gotta get food!"

"That stinks," I said. "My brother got drafted. He's dead now. That's why I came up with a foolproof way to get out of it if the draft officers come calling. If you let me leave with my money and clock, I'll tell you. I won't even demand to take a hostage with me."

"She's lying!" the girl behind me squeaked. "Let's kill her!"

"You're way too violent for your age," I informed her. "You sound about six or seven. You should be at least eight before you threaten people with knives."

"Pleeeeeease!" the boy who had my new knife to his neck cried. "Just let her go and have her tell us! I don't want to die!"

I smiled. "You're a smart kid."

"Shut up!" the young man snarled. There was hope as well as fear in his eyes. "All right. Tell us the secret. If it's good enough, then we'll let you go."

"With my money and my clock?" I asked.

He paused. "Sure."

"I don't like that pause. I don't trust that pause. You will let me go first, and *then* I'll tell you."

"Just kill her!" the little girl shouted. "She's lying!"

There was a long, long pause, with everybody breathing heavily. I could hear my heart pounding in my ears.

I couldn't think in all this silence. But I had to keep my mouth shut. They were desperate. They would weaken if I made them wait long enough. That was obvious. Completely evident. No doubt about it.

"Alternately, here's another idea —" I began.

"Shut up!" the young man yelled.

"If I were capable of that, I would've done it," I said. "Believe me, I wish I had. Anyway, why don't you let me just take the clock? Not a hostage; not the money. Then, once I'm at the end of the street, I'll tell you the secret."

"All right," the young man said with a sly smile. "Go ahead."

"I don't like that sly smile," I said warily. "What do you know that I don't?"

"Only what I'll do to you if it turns out you're lying." His smile gleamed. "I'm a fast runner, and that clock looks heavy."

"You have an uncomfortable point." I sighed. "It's a good thing I'm not lying. All right. I'll move away from my hostage as soon as that knife is gone from my back. Scary little girl, move away, please."

The sharpness poking through the back of my dress, thankfully, receded.

I breathed a sigh of relief and hefted the clock into my arms. "It's not nearly as heavy as it looks," I muttered under my breath as I inched away from the criminals. "And I'm good at running while carrying heavy things. Did they think this was my first time having somebody attempt to rob me? Good thing they didn't think to demand the knife back. That's worth at least as much as the coppers they stole from me."

I walked to the end of the street and glanced hopefully both ways down the new street I was facing, looking for guards or at least witnesses. There were none, unfortunately.

There was, however, a boy who looked about eight years old waiting off to the left with a knife in his hand.

I groaned. "How many hardened criminals are *in* your family?"

The young man grinned. "Enough. The foolproof secret?"

Yeah, I'd totally been lying. Thankfully, I was good at improvising. "Well, when they ask you what your age is, you lie."

"They keep records!" the young man shouted. "Are you stupid?!"

"No, they don't!" I shot back. "The draft officers can't read! They just make it look like they can by scribbling nonsense down! Think about it! Do they *look* like they're rich enough to have learned?!"

Startled, the four siblings looked at one another, probably trying to gauge whether this was the truth.

"Well, bye!"

I took the split second opportunity to bolt to the right. Then, knowing yelling for help probably wouldn't do any good on a street like this, I screamed at the top of my lungs, "Somebody's throwing free money around out here!"

Windows and doors flung open all around me. People scrambled outside to see where the money was, crowding in the way of my furious pursuers, who starting shouting and cursing. Screams followed when a woman noticed those children had knives, screams came from the kids as a nasty-faced man tackled the girl to steal her knife, and the confusion caused just enough distraction for me to find a garbage receptacle out of sight of my pursuers and vault into it, my heart pounding.

I waited for several minutes, which was torture because I didn't dare think any louder than a mutter. But at last, I peeked out of the top to make sure they were gone and climbed out, heaving the clock with me. I made sure to walk down only main streets that had guard stations dotted across them for the rest of the journey home.

"The back of your dress is cut!" Ma cried as soon as I walked in. "Did someone pull a knife out on you again?!"

"Just a little one."

"*HENINA!*"

"Don't be so overprotective, Ma." I grinned, setting the clock on the floor. It would be worth a lot of money after Pa finished fixing it, so I had no regrets. "I've never been killed yet, after all."

SIX SHINY SILVER COINS AND THE RIDICULOUS RUCKUS THEY CAUSED

"And I want one of these," Ma was saying, pointing to a fresh basket of apples by the stall. "No, not that one! The one that's *not* overripe. There."

The fruit seller looked a little sulky as Ma firmly picked up the largest apple, which had no pocks or worm holes, and deposited it in her bag. "That'll be two coppers, fifteen irons, and three quarter-irons," the fruit seller said.

"No, it won't," I said promptly. "It'll be two coppers, twelve irons, and one half-iron. I kept a running total of the prices. Come to think of it, since you cheated Ma out of three irons and a half-iron last week, that means she only owes you two coppers and nine irons now."

The fruit seller looked offended.

"Henina," Ma said, pointing to the opposite end of the market square, "why don't you go over there?"

"I'll ignore that unsubtle hint, primarily because she's cheating you and it's irking me," I said.

The fruit seller was looking mad.

"Henina," Ma said sharply.

"The price has now changed," the apple seller said in a tight voice. "You now owe me three coppers."

"Oh, big deal, it's a quarter-iron difference," I said.

"Henina!" Ma snapped. "Go over there and stop pestering me!"

"I wasn't pestering you, I was correcting that woman's morality or mathematics, one of the two, though perhaps it's both. She could be stupid *and* crooked."

"Three coppers, one iron," the fruit seller said.

"*Henina!*" Ma shouted.

"Okay, fine, I'll go over there," I said.

I wandered off towards the other end of the market square. Above us, the king's soothsayer stepped out onto the castle balcony, surveying the crowd slowly and with a self-important air. I looked around and saw hundreds of fortune tellers and soothsayers settling down at the edges of the square with a palpable air of expectation.

"Oh, right, it's Prophecy Day," I said. "The Fates could do a better job of making it interesting."

Somebody jostled me and stepped on my foot.

"Ow!" I complained.

"Sorry," the man said, not looking back.

"You're not acting like it," I said, but he was already gone.

A loud, thundering drum solo began, and the soothsayers and fortune tellers around the edges of the market stood. The drum continued, loud and repetitive and insistent, marking the beginning of a glorious new Prophecy Day.

"Or a boring one," I said. "Half the time all the Fates do is foretell the weather, or they do something trivial. There's a reason most people don't even bother to come to the square. Well, two reasons, since you can hear the prophecy from any fortune teller or soothsayer in the entire kingdom, but . . ."

A little girl raced past me, giggling as she stamped on my foot.

"Hey!" I shouted.

Too late. She was past me, racing after a little boy.

I sighed. "Okay, fine, since you're a child, I'll excuse you."

The drum kept going on and on. There seemed to be no stop to it. I squinted up at the sky, and it was the right time, but the drum just kept on going.

"Are the Fates waiting for the king to show up?" I muttered, looking up at the balcony. "I can't believe he's late. That's so rude. Maybe he doesn't respect them, either. I can't blame him for not taking Prophecy Day seriously, since it's always so . . . OW!"

A huge, heavy man had stepped on my foot.

"Watch it!" I shouted.

"Oh, sorry," he said, moving aside.

"At least somebody feels some remorse," I fumed. "This is ridiculous."

The king appeared on the balcony, closely followed by the king's fortune teller. He stood there, the sunlight glinting off his impressive crown, and then the drum abruptly stopped.

Lightning sliced out of a clear sky to strike the top spire of the castle.

Then it did it again.

"Yep, the Fates were waiting for the king," I nodded. "They seem to think he's more important than he thinks them . . ."

But my voice was drowned out before I could finish thinking. The mouth of every soothsayer and fortune teller opened, and a roar of words poured out in unison in hundreds of different voices.

"The Fates see all and hear all. The king will perform a great act of generosity before the sun sets this day."

The tide of voices stopped.

"Huh, no weather predictions," I said. "And the king looks positively horrified. I'm guessing this wasn't something he expected. Oh, now he's grabbing his purse —"

"As a great act of generosity to you, my people," the king bellowed, "whoever catches these silvers may keep them!"

He flung one out into the crowd. It glinted in the air for a brief moment as everyone held their breath. Then it plunged down into the center of the crowd.

Pandemonium reigned.

Hundreds of people scrambled for the silver coin, and there were shouts and screams as several fought over it.

"I would have tried for it, but it was too far away," I murmured. "Besides, he said 'these silvers.' That means . . ."

Sure enough, the king threw out a second coin.

Fervor and desperation surged through the crowd as a second mass of people raced and clawed to reach the new one.

"Still too far away," I murmured. "Come on . . . come on . . ."

The king threw a third coin in the air. The silver glinted up at the sun in blinding light. A dozen people were already moving, but I had figured out where it would land first and was there before them.

Bam!

I caught the coin in both hands and kept on running.

People screamed and dashed after me. Someone grabbed the back of my shirt. I kicked back with my foot, and somebody stepped on it.

"Another one!" I screamed, jabbing my finger in the air to point.

Six Shiny Silver Coins and the Ridiculous Ruckus They Caused

The person who'd grabbed the back of my shirt looked up, and that was all the opening I needed. I twisted out of his grip and dashed through the crowd, fist clenched tightly around my prize, determined to get away before anybody stole it from me.

Screams flew through the air as a fourth coin was thrown. I reached the edge of the square. Then the fifth coin.

A man tackled me from behind and tried to seize the coin from my hand. I bit his fingers, hard. He shouted and shoved me, but I'd already stomped hard on the instep of his foot.

The man screamed, "Stop! She's getting away!" But he was drowned out by the other pandemonium and screaming as the sixth coin was thrown.

I dodged into a back alleyway, one of the ones I was most familiar with, and vaulted up into a garbage receptacle, not even checking to see what was inside it. Luck wasn't with me, because it was filled with putrid kitchen scraps, but at least it made for a soft landing.

I waited with my heart hammering, trying not to think of anything, because when I thought, I tended to say things. I wasn't very good at controlling my mouth.

"Come on . . . come on . . ." I murmured.

The ridiculous ruckus continued for over an hour, until finally it settled down enough that it seemed like it might be safe to emerge from my stinking hiding place. I poked my head up above the top to make sure nobody was coming, saw an empty alleyway, and tucked the silver coin into the hidden pocket under my armpit before hopping down and landing easily, despite the distance.

I'd had a lot of practice vaulting into and out of garbage receptacles. Finding broken things for Pa to fix and sell was my job.

"I wonder what I'll buy with it," I mused as I walked. "It's a whole silver coin, after all. Enough to almost cover my family's rent for a month. Which is what Ma will want to use it for, but no way am I going to give it to her . . ."

Three familiar-looking scamps poked their heads out of a garbage receptacle I was passing.

"You've got a silver coin?" a blond-haired little boy asked.

"I've never seen one before," a little girl with short black hair announced, her eyes glittering.

"If only we had one, we could afford to eat," a skinny brown-haired boy sniffled.

All three street children immediately looked pitiful.

I snorted. "Right, like I'm going to fall for that one. What'd you find?"

"A broken chair," black-haired Arbin said shrewdly, her eyes calculatingly eyeing my hidden pocket, which she had, unfortunately, noticed a few days ago. "We can sell it to you for a silver coin."

"Which is only a hundred times more than the chair is worth," I said.

"Exactly!" the blond-haired Jorvis said. "A bargain!"

"Math isn't your strong suit, is it?" I asked. "I didn't hire you scamps to cheat me, I hired you to root through garbage. Come on, let's get the chair out."

The three heads disappeared down into the garbage receptacle, and soon the chair had crashed to the ground, splitting a relatively-intact piece of furniture into three splintered pieces.

"Impressive lack of technique," I said. "The chair's now worth a whole lot less than it would have been worth a minute ago."

"You mean, it's only worth a tin now?" Dobbel asked hopefully.

"Ha," I said. "You wish. I pay you in food, not money. Come on, bring the chair, and we'll take it back to Pa to see what he thinks it's worth."

Grumbling, the three children each gathered up a part of the chair — Jorbin picked up the seat, Arbin collected the legs, and Dobbel clutched the split back in front of him — then we headed down the back alleyways, studiously ignoring other street children we passed. It was best to turn a blind eye to whatever they were up to. Most of them worked for the crime lords when they weren't working for me, which was one of the reasons why the crime lords and my family had, ah, a rather touchy relationship.

"Oh, but that reminds me," I called to one of them as we passed. "Craiga, Ma noticed that you stole her cooking pan last week, and she's really mad! You'd better bring something spectacular next time you come, or she might refuse to feed you!"

The dirty-blond boy looked so crestfallen at this news that I had to stop and clap him on the shoulder.

"That's what happens when you steal from the hand that feeds you. Don't worry, kid, we'll get her to forgive you. Just don't do it again. Or *you*, either," I added to Arbin, grabbing her hand that had snaked into my pocket while my arm was extended.

"But I've never even *seen* one before!" she said sulkily.

By the time we got back home, Ma was preparing lunch with her new produce, and she greeted me with wild excitement.

"You caught a coin, didn't you?" she cried, beckoning me in. "I saw it! Imagine what we can do with a whole silver to spare!"

"You seem to be assuming I'll share," I said.

Ma put her hands on her hips. "Of course you'll share! What would you do with a whole silver?"

"Anything I want to," I said.

The crooked little scamps followed me through the house into the back room that Pa used for his workshop. I watched Ma retrieve a dishtowel from Dorrel as he tried to stuff it in his pocket.

"Clever, but not clever enough," I told him. "You've gotta only steal stuff that nobody will miss."

Ma looked indignant.

"Okay, don't steal from us at all," I said.

Dorrel looked vaguely pouty.

"Ah, our gatherers," Pa said, smiling at the children.

All three of them brightened and beamed at him. Most of the crooked little scamps we employed to root through garbage weren't fond of Ma, despite the fact that she was the one who fed them, because she treated them with great suspicion. Well-deserved suspicion, but that didn't mean they liked it. They all loved Pa.

"And what have you got for me today?" Pa asked, smiling broadly. He glanced at the pieces of what they were holding, and a faint look of confusion crossed his face.

"It's a chair," Dorrel said proudly, holding up the split back.

"Ah, right," Pa said with obvious relief. "Yes. Of course it is. How kind of you to bring it to me to repair."

"It'd be more kind if they hadn't broken it in the first place," I said.

"We did not!" Arbin protested. "It was in the garbage anyway!"

"If we break rich people's things on purpose, could we get extra pay for that?" the skinny Dorrel asked in great excitement.

"No," Ma said immediately. "In fact, you'd probably be caught by the guards and sent to the battlefront."

"He's not twelve yet," I said. "He's too young to be drafted."

"I'm *almost* twelve," Dorrel said proudly.

"Well, don't admit it," I said. "When the census takers ask, you lie your head off."

"I've told them I'm six for four years now," Jorvis bragged.

"Attaboy," I said, grinning. My older brother had been killed in the war. I had no love for the draft.

"Which reminds me," Ma said, straightening. "Henina caught a silver coin today!"

"How did that remind you of the coin?" I asked. "It sounds like you were just looking for a good excuse to broach the subject."

Pa's brow furrowed. "'Caught'?"

"The king threw six of them into the crowd," Ma said importantly. "He said that anybody who caught one could keep it."

"Yeah, and I caught it, which means it's mine to do with as I please," I said.

"It would be nice to have an entire silver to spare," Pa said, his eyes going distant. "We could invest in higher-end tools, buy you a new cooking pan . . ."

"Or you can stop daydreaming about my money, which I am not going to share," I said flatly. "I might buy a dog."

"No pets!" Ma shouted. "We can barely afford to feed ourselves!"

I snorted. "Yeah, we're not that desperate. But I'll grant that one silver doesn't cover a continuing expense. I know! I could buy a book, maybe even two. If I can find two short ones, a silver might cover two —"

"A book!" Ma exploded. "What use would that be?! You'd memorize it in one reading, and the rest of us would have no use for it at all!"

"You have a point, but maybe I could convince Veiet and Dorry to learn," I said.

"No," Ma grated. "Useless skills that only rich people care about are not worth the time. And something like that would certainly not be worth the expense."

"I'm feeling a little irritated that you think you can tell me how to spend my money," I said.

"You're so selfish!" Ma exclaimed.

"Yes!" I said cheerfully. "Altruistic people get taken advantage of."

And then I realized something. I realized exactly how to spend my money.

I headed purposefully for the front door.

"Where are you going?" Ma demanded, hands on her hips.

"Outside," I said, opening the front door.

"You're going out to spend it, aren't you?!" she shouted, charging after me. "Don't you dare!"

I ducked through the door and raced out into the street before she could stop me. Glancing back over my shoulder, I saw Ma waving her arms as she chased after me, and Pa and the three street kids watching from the doorway. Pa looked worried, and the three scamps looked ecstatic at the entertainment.

I ducked around a corner, hid behind a neighbor's water barrel, and waited for Ma to run past, yelling my name. Then I slipped up to the door and pushed it open.

Inside the house was gloom, lit by many candles. The scribe who lived there didn't like distraction, so he always kept the windows closed. The room smelled musty, lacking for fresh air.

"Almost done," he muttered, not looking up from the book he was illustrating. "Just need another few days."

"I'm not your customer, Rorrl," I said. "It's me. Henina."

He squinted and looked up at me through the gloom. "I don't have any spare books here. I've sold them all. And you've read another copy of this one already."

"I know," I said. "I glanced at the page. It's the one about the war. Are you doing well?"

"Never have enough time to finish," he mumbled, stretching his fingers, which were looking crabbed and tight. "Always rushing. Always rushing. Wish I could afford to take my time on a project and produce something really quality, for once."

"Good," I said. "Well, not good, so don't look at me incredulously, but I have a solution for you. Here."

I pulled the single silver coin from my hidden pocket. It glimmered in the firelight.

"It's silver," I said unnecessarily. "Not tin."

"I know," he murmured. "My customers regularly pay in silver."

"Huh," I said. "I didn't think about that, but of course they do. That's about how much a short book copied over is worth."

He nodded, his eyes drooping with weariness.

"Well, this is for you," I said, holding out the coin to him. "So you can take extra time if you need to. If you want to. Or you can just take a break."

He shook his head slowly. "It's . . . thoughtful," he murmured. "But I don't take things for nothing, and I don't have time to fit in an extra book."

I put the silver coin firmly on his desk.

"I'm paying you for teaching me how to read all those years ago," I said. "Nobody else could have taught me."

The firelight flickered in the shininess of the coin.

"You didn't need much help," he said. "You basically figured it out on your own."

"All the same," I said.

He stared at the coin for a moment, and then nodded, slowly. "You have my th—"

"No," I said abruptly. "Don't thank me. It makes me feel altruistic, and ughhhh. Don't tell Ma or Pa either, will you? If they find out, they're bound to attempt to take it back, and it's my coin to do with what I please."

He smiled faintly. "I'm not sure you're capable of keeping secrets."

"I've kept secrets before!" I said indignantly. "Sometimes for days at a time before I let them slip out!"

He chuckled.

"Henina!" I heard Ma shouting outside, her voice getting louder. She was walking back down this way again. "Henina, get back here!"

"Well, I'm off to spend the day around the city, so that Ma will think I frivolously spent it all by the time I get home," I said cheerfully. "I'm thinking I'll tell her I've spent it all on food. Extremely gourmet food. A shocking indulgence to eat an entire silver's worth of food in one day. She'll be pretty outraged." The idea amused me.

"Henina!" I heard her voice shouting outside as she walked past. "Henina!"

"Well, bye then," I said quickly, ducking out the back door and racing down the back street.

There was a one-armed former soldier slumped against a building, holding out a cup to beg for coins. The cup was empty, and he'd obviously fallen asleep. I waited until nobody was watching and then dropped three iron coins in his cup.

"That's enough for a meal," I murmured. "Everyone deserves to eat."

Then I hurried off into the alleyways before he could wake.

"That's the thing about altruism," I told myself. "As long as nobody can see me do it, it's okay."

Seven Shameless Scamps Looking Pitiful

"She found a silver coin!" a child cried, pointing at me.
"Silver coin?!" another shrieked.
"Silver coin?"
"Silver coin!"
"Silver coin?!"
"Silver coin?"
"Silver coin!!"
Seven shameless scamps followed me, holding out their hands.
"Sorry," I said cheerfully. "I spent it all on gourmet food and ate it."
They stopped dead, staring at me, aghast.
"Mmmmm," I added mischievously.
"HOW COULD YOU?!" seven voices screamed.
"It was the will of the Fates," I said loftily. "I had to. The Fates said I would. It was prophesied."
"IT WAS NOT!"
I snickered. I loved to mess with people who deserved it.

Thirteen Years After a Sister's Wedding

"Congratulations on your engagement," I told my sister. "But shouldn't you have let the Fates pick?"

"I have no idea what you're talking about," Carran said loftily.

"You know, with the stones. The way you encouraged Elayn to do."

"I never did any such thing."

"Oh, right. So what you're saying is, you *didn't* babble about how romantic it would be to let fortune tellers pick her marriage for her? Good to know my memory's wrong about that, although it's never been wrong about anything before."

"Maaaaaaa! Henina's being rude!" she shouted.

Ma called down the hallway, "This isn't news!"

Fifteen Problems in One Hundred Words

"Henina," Ma said, "think *silently*, for once, while I buy our produce."
I was bad at that, but okay.
The roof was leaking, Pa'd hurt his hand, an employee was stealing from us, four more wanted to, I'd lost a necklace, Ma needed new cookware, I'd run out of books, my brothers were annoying, the weather was rainy, I'd missed breakfast, I didn't want apples, I was feeling cranky, my shoe was too tight, I had a rock in it too, and that apple seller was overcharging Ma right now.
"You said all that out loud," Ma said with exasperation.

Author's Notes

Ogre in Boots

Do you remember the scene in *Black Magic Academy* when Rulisa said she got sent to an ogre who tried to eat her, so she turned him into a cat and gave him to a miller's family to raise?

Well, that was always meant as a subtle "Puss in Boots" reference, one of the many fairy tales I snuck into that series. (Grin.) But of course, that didn't show the end of the fairy tale, in which the ogre-turned-cat would quite naturally show up to get revenge on Rulisa, and meet Rulisa's even-less-nice father instead!

So I wrote it as a standaloneable short story, which clearly had to be from Rulisa's father's point of view because he's hilarious. I wrote it at around the time I was writing *Black Magic Academy*, then rewrote it many years later, a few months before starting *White Magic Academy*, as part of my efforts to make sure I was getting the feel of the series right.

See, there were seven years in between books, and I know how easy it is for authors to get the feel of a series wrong if there's a large gap between writing books in the same series. So I worked very hard to try to prevent that problem. I hope I succeeded!

An Alternate Solution to the Sleeping Curse
Puss in Oops
Entrance Interview

The first two are drabble versions of "On the Way Through the Woods" and "Ogre in Boots" (sort of) that I wrote on a whim years ago. The third is a brand new drabble that I wrote specifically for this book. All things considered, I think Rulisa's father's reputation is the only reason she got in to that school!

The Weeds within the Rulership

In 2016, when I was planning to sell books at a convention, I had a brainwave. I would write a tie-in short story for three of my four series ("On the Way Through the Woods" already existed), and then print all four out and include them in a binder, so that people looking at my books at the table could see if they liked the style of a particular series by reading something short and self-contained!

Unfortunately, like so many things, it was a better idea in theory than in practice. Nobody really cared about the binder of short stories, because they could simply read the first few pages of the book that they were, you know, considering buying.

Despite that, I enjoyed the process so much that I decided to write at least one tie-in short story for every series. It turned out to be a fun way to turn minor characters into protagonists, or to allow the usual protagonists to face smaller conflicts than in a book.

The Secrets from the Rulership

In 2018, when I unwisely joined yet another multi-author box set (you'll find that most of my most head-slappingly stupid moments as a writer from 2016-2018 start with these words), we were required to include some kind of exclusive and brand new content that was connected to the nonexclusive book we were including, as an incentive for previous readers of those books to want to pick it up.

That box set, *Storms of Fate and Fury*, ended after six months, so we got the rights to our exclusive content back. This was mine.

You see, the book I had included was *The Keeper and the Rulership*, and I'd been thinking about writing a short story from the Ruler's point of view for years, so that seemed like a perfect choice. The thing that makes her such an interesting antagonist is that she's not really a villain — she tends to be less right than the main character (Raneh), but she's generally not wrong.

The Numbers across the Rulership

I love Hurik. He's such a stubborn nonconformist, although he does have a few minor character flaws such as, you know, laziness.

When I wrote the earliest draft of *The Keeper and the Rulership*, there was a major arc in which it was revealed that Hurik had already learned mathematics and was practicing it in secret, despite the serious dangers of doing so. This was meant to underline the dangers Raneh was in because of her forbidden magic, and it worked in the earliest drafts to lead to a climax. But eventually, when I wrote the final draft, the book just . . . didn't need that. There was no good reason for Hurik to confide in Raneh. And there was no good reason for him to ever get found out, either. So Hurik's taking of the oath simply happened offscreen while the main character was gone.

There were a lot of things I said "Good riddance!" to from the early drafts (such as a hideously badly written rival for Raneh), but Hurik's arc was the one thing I missed. My idea for his arc was actually the thing that originally triggered the whole plot, so losing it was sad.

So, a tie-in short story was in order! In my earliest drafts, I called it "When the Magic Died," and I still love that title, but there were two problems with it. First: it didn't match the naming pattern of the rest of the series (which I excused by saying, "Well, Hurik doesn't follow other people's patterns, so there!"). Second and more importantly, though . . . the plot of the short story kind of had nothing to do with magic dying, so the title became irrelevant.

My favorite thing about the short story was that I was able to fit in the actual words for the numbers in the Rulership, and show what they're like from a linguistic standpoint. That was awesome.

The Novice at the Rulership
The Painting like the Rulership

I figured I ought to give Yaika something from her point of view, so I gave her two drabbles. I'm so generous. (Laugh.)

Fairy Feet

This is the tie-in short story I wrote for the Fairy Senses series to go in that binder. It's set in between chapters twelve and thirteen of *Fairy Barometer*, the fourth book in the series. I thought it would be fun to tell the story of how Maricela met Big Feet, since it happened offscreen. I made Daisy the viewpoint character because I knew she would still be struggling with jealousy after her book, and it felt like she deserved a little something extra to make up for it. (You'll note that I also gave her something special at the end of *Fairy Crown*.)

Fairy Fingers
Fairy Stink

The first drabble exists because I wanted to give Davis the chance to get the better of Sunflower. The second was a deleted scene from *Fairy Perfume* that I wanted to keep somewhere!

Dragon's Dawn

This is the tie-in short story I wrote for the Dragon Eggs series to go in that binder. It's set in between *Dragon's Egg* and *Dragon's Hope* (the first and second books in the series).

Dragon's Yowl

I wanted to write something from Henry's point of view, but I only had enough of a plot idea to make a drabble. I'll probably write more tie-in short stories for this series later.

Trials of a Teenage Shapeshifter

Back around 1998, when I was in high school, I wrote a book called *By Moonlight* about a teenage girl who became a werewolf. Then she discovered that her best friend from elementary school, who had just moved back into town, was a vampire. It wasn't very good, so I tucked it away. Then, in 2017, remembering that character, I wrote this drabble. Well, then I *had* to turn it into a book, didn't I?!

Triumph of a Teenage Werevulture

In 2017, when I unwisely joined yet another multi-author box set (told ya), *Trials of a Teenage Werevulture* went straight from *Spellbound* and into *Marked by Fate*. In order to give my readers who preordered *Marked by Fate* something special, I wrote this short story as a present that was exclusive to people who preordered for a few months.

Maybe if I'd spent half as much time and money marketing my own books as other people's, I would've, like, actually managed to make money on my books instead of losing money for three years straight. Y'think?

Trials of a Teenage Zombie

I met a man at an event who was not only a paleontologist, but *also* an expert in vultures and dodos. I pumped his brain for about two hours straight. (My friend Candice, who was with me, was awfully patient about that conversation she had no interest in . . .)

This drabble came about as a direct result of that conversation. He said that vultures love the heart and lungs of an animal (they're like candy), and they're also fond of guts. Falcons prefer brains.

My immediate reaction was, "Why has nobody ever written a book about a zombie werefalcon?!"

Naturally that wouldn't fit in this series's worldbuilding, but I could have members of the two species fighting over a brain. (Grin.)

One Silly Chatterbox That Won't Stop Talking

This was the second tie-in short story I wrote for The Numbers Just Keep Getting Bigger series. I thought it would be fun to show Henina's past, as mentioned in *Twenty-Four Potential Children of Prophecy*. We got to meet Rorrl in "Six Shiny Silver Coins and the Ridiculous Ruckus They Caused," which was the first tie-in short story I wrote for the series, and I thought it would be sweet to show how patient he was with Henina at the beginning.

THREE LITTLE STONES THAT SAID THE WRONG THING

After finishing that short story, I started wondering, "What other interesting things would have happened in Henina's life while she was growing up?" And I had the idea of having something happen at her oldest sister's wedding. It took awhile to figure out how Henina would be relevant to that story, but once I did, it turned into a very interesting tidbit about the Fate-centered culture she grew up in.

FOUR HARDENED CRIMINALS ON A DANGEROUS STREET

Henina's sense of self-preservation is not, shall we say, high enough to stop her from doing anything she feels like doing. That's probably why most people aren't as successful at salvage as she is.

SIX SHINY SILVER COINS AND THE RIDICULOUS RUCKUS THEY CAUSED

In 2016, when I unwisely joined yet another multi-author box set (See?! See?!), I wrote this tie-in short story to promote *Myths and Legends*, which *Twenty-Four Potential Children of Prophecy* was in.

The part at the beginning where people start coincidentally stepping on Henina's foot every time she's saying something insulting about the Fates is the moment she first caught the attention of the Fates. Her complaints annoyed them, and that was why they came up with the "act of great generosity" prophecy. When they saw the enthusiastic response to that prophecy, the Fates decided to do something even more exciting the next month. So yes, Henina brought it all on herself. She is directly at fault for the prophecy she gets wrapped up in.

Seven Shameless Scamps Looking Pitiful
Thirteen Years After a Sister's Wedding
Fifteen Problems in One Hundred Words

I pretty much wrote these drabbles just to fill the last few pages of this short story collection! (Yes, I'm shameless.)

About the Author

Emily Martha Sorensen has written over forty fantasy books that are funny and clean. For awhile, she had a tendency to join way too many multi-author box sets instead of finishing the series she had already (facepalm), but she's recovered her sanity.

She has four kids, a wonderful husband who is the greatest ever, and eight series that she is DEFINITELY GOING TO FINISH SOME OF before she starts the next one, even though the next one has been making faces and taunting her.

She wonders why she's writing this in the third person. Has she *really* recovered her sanity, or have the kids driven her batty? Guess she'll find out if she's now a werebat at the full moon . . .

Milton Keynes UK
Ingram Content Group UK Ltd.
UKHW040137170224
437973UK00001B/81